CHRISTMAS FAIRY TALES

CHRISTMAS FAIRY TALES

Selected by Neil Philip

Illustrated by Isabelle Brent

LITTLE, BROWN AND COMPANY

Boston   New York   Toronto   London

A LITTLE, BROWN BOOK
First published in Great Britain
by Little, Brown and Company (UK)
Conceived, designed and produced by
The Albion Press Limited
Spring Hill, Idbury, Oxfordshire OX7 6RU

SPELLING: In this anthology we have retained British spelling
in British texts and American spelling in American texts.

ISBN 0-316-87836-7

A CIP catalogue record for this book is available from the British Library

Designer: Emma Bradford
Project Manager: Elizabeth Wilkes

1 3 5 7 9 8 6 4 2

Typesetting by York House Typographic, London
Colour origination by York House Graphics, London
Printed and bound in Hong Kong by South China Printing Co

Little, Brown and Company (UK)
Brettenham House
Lancaster Place
London WC2E 7EN

FOR SOPHIE CLAIRE FISHER
I.B.
FOR JESSICA AND CHARLOTTE GIBLING
N.P.

CONTENTS

INTRODUCTION

NEIL PHILIP

Fairy tales and Christmas are natural companions, for the keynotes of both are magic, wonder, and joy.

This book collects twelve Christmas fairy tales from around the world, each of which offers a wise insight into the true meaning of Christmas. Some of them are funny, and some are sad, but all leave an afterglow of hope for the future, and that is the essential Christmas message.

It is no accident that three stories of the twelve are written by one man, Hans Christian Andersen. Born into a poor family in Denmark in 1805, Andsersen virtually invented the modern fairy tale, and remains its greatest master. The three stories I have chosen show him at his most thoughtful. The little fir tree in "The Fir Tree," who cannot enjoy the present because it is always anticipating the future, and the old oak tree in "The Last Dream of the Old Oak Tree," who discovers that nothing we love can be lost, show how deftly Andersen translated human truths into fairy tale terms.

"The Book of Fairy Tales" is a more complex story, with a social message as well as a spiritual one. Its belief in the redemptive power of stories themselves is central to Andersen, and for this reason I have discarded the tale's usual title, "The Cripple," and returned to Andersen's own first choice, "The Book of Fairy Tales."

Most of the other authors in this collection were inspired by Andersen, and his influence can be seen particularly in "The Poor Count's Christmas," and "The Best That Life Has to Give," by the American authors Frank Stockton and Howard Pyle. A third American, the renowned storyteller Ruth Sawyer, offers one of the liveliest of all Christmas tales, in her own unique voice: "Schnitzle, Schnotzle, and Schnootzle." Her exuberance is well matched by the wit of Norwegian author Alf Prøysen in his story "Father Christmas and the Carpenter."

Frances Browne's "The Christmas Cuckoo" comes from her novel *Granny's Wonderful Chair,* which is full of intense, visionary tales. You would never guess that their Irish author had been blind since infancy.

"The Story of a Cat" by Mary de Morgan (sister of the famous Pre-Raphaelite ceramic designer William de Morgan) is in some ways Dickens's *A Christmas Carol* in miniature, and shares some of the atmosphere and power of that great work. Mary de Morgan was probably the best of all Hans Christian Andersen's followers in England, and her fairy tales are unfairly neglected today.

Two of the stories are from folk tradition: the comic Norwegian folktale "Why the Sea is Salt," and the enchanting Russian legend of "Babushka and the Three Wise Men."

And, of course, I had to include that most classic of all Christmas fairy tales, E. T. A. Hoffmann's "The Nutcracker." This is most familiar today from the ballet by Tchaikovsky, which was in fact based on a French adaptation of Hoffmann's tale by Alexander Dumas. For my shortened retelling, I have returned to Hoffmann's original tale.

In all twelve of these tales, the generous spirit of Christmas can be felt at work. In that spirit, I will close with a thirteenth fairy tale — a true one, this time.

Several years ago, I was in New York City just before Christmas. That's the time when New York looks its best, with the trees all strung with lights, and the great Christmas tree in Rockefeller Plaza casting its blessing over the bustling streets. The whole city seems to hum.

My wife, Emma, and I went into a store looking for Christmas gifts to bring home to England. It's a tiny shop, tucked into a sliver of space between bigger stores, and it sells all kinds of wind-up toys, from little plastic pieces of fun to real works of art.

As we browsed, we noticed an elderly man who was also looking round the shelves. He was big, and round, with white hair and a flowing white beard, and he was dressed in a red jacket and red jeans. I nudged Emma, and said, "Look who else is here!"

Later, I noticed the man talking to the assistant at the counter. She was a young woman, maybe nineteen or twenty.

When we went to make our purchases, she was trembling. She turned to me, and said, "I can't believe it. Santa Claus was in the store!" Her voice was low with wonder, and light was welling from her eyes.

I asked her, "Did he buy anything?"

"No," she replied. "But he gave me this." She held out a golden ring, set with a sparkling red stone. "He took my hand, and put this in it, and said, 'May all your dreams come true.'"

At that moment, her colleague came out of the back room, and she told her that Santa Claus had visited the store, and had said he would return. The colleague laughed, and said, "Oh, sure! He won't be back."

The girl turned, and quickly, fiercely, with a blazing intensity, said, "Yes, he will. *Santa Claus doesn't tell lies.*"

Now it may be that the ring was plastic and glass, and the man in the toy store a practical joker. But I don't think so, and nor did the girl to whom he gave the ring.

Christmas is the time when magic can happen, as this collection of Christmas fairy tales shows. It's a time when the hardest-hearted Scrooge has the chance to act and think for once like a real human being: to give a stranger a gift, and whisper, "May all your dreams come true."

THE BOOK OF FAIRY TALES

HANS CHRISTIAN ANDERSEN

English version by Neil Philip

There was an old manor house with a dashing young squire. He and his wife enjoyed their wealth and fortune, and liked to share it with others. They wanted everybody to be as happy as they were.

On Christmas Eve, a beautifully decorated Christmas tree stood in the great hall. A fire was burning in the hearth, and the frames of the family portraits were hung with branches of fir. Here the master and mistress and their guests would sing and dance the night away.

Earlier in the evening, Christmas was celebrated in the servants' hall. Here, too, stood a big Christmas tree glittering with red and white candles, and trimmed with little Danish flags, and swans and fishing nets cut out of paper and filled with candy. The poor children from the village had all been invited. Their mothers came too, but they weren't interested in the tree so much as the tables laden with Christmas presents: useful woollens and linen to make dresses and trousers. Only the little children stretched out their hands to the candles, the tinsel, and the flags.

They had come early in the afternoon, and they all got some Christmas pudding, as well as roast goose and red cabbage. Then when they'd all admired the Christmas tree, and the presents had been handed out, they all had a little glass of punch and some apple cake.

When they got back to their own poor cottages, they all said, "That's what I call the good life," and sat back to digest their meal, and have a proper look at their presents.

Now one couple was called Garden-Kirsten and Garden-Ole. They both worked in the manor house garden, weeding and digging, and that kept a roof over their heads and bread in their mouths. Every Christmas they got their share of presents. They had five children, and the squire's generosity clothed them all.

"They're kind-hearted folk, the master and mistress," they would say. "But, of course, they can afford it, and it makes them feel good."

"Here are some good hard-wearing clothes for the four youngest," said Ole, "but isn't there anything for poor Hans? They don't usually forget him, even though he can't come to the party."

Hans was their eldest son. When he was small he'd been the quickest and liveliest child, but then he suddenly went "wobbly" in the legs, and couldn't stand or walk. For five years now he had been bedridden.

"Well, I did get something for him," said his mother, "but it's nothing really — just a book for him to read."

"A fat lot of use that will be to him," said his father.

But Hans was pleased with it. He was a very bright boy, who liked reading. Even though he had to lie in bed, he did what work he could, knitting socks and even bedspreads; the mistress of the manor had praised his work, and bought some.

It was a book of fairy tales that Hans had been given, with lots to read, and lots to think about.

"There's not much use for that sort of thing in this house," said his parents. "Still, let him read. It passes the time, and he can't always be knitting."

Spring came. The flowers came up in the garden, and so did the weeds, which meant there was plenty of work for the gardener and his apprentices, and also for Garden-Kirsten and Garden-Ole.

"It's nothing but wasted effort," they both said. "As soon as we've raked the paths out, they get messed up again, what with the endless visitors they have at the manor. Just think of the cost! But the master and mistress are rich enough."

"It's a funny old world," said Ole. "The parson says we are all God's children. Why is it so unfair?"

"It's because of the Fall," said Kirsten.

They talked it over again that evening, while Hans lay in bed reading his book of fairy tales.

Drudgery had hardened their hands, and poverty had blunted their minds. They couldn't make it out; they weren't up to it. As they talked they got more and more hot and bothered.

"Some people are rich and happy, while others just scrape by. Why should we suffer just because Adam and Eve were disobedient and inquisitive? We would never have behaved like those two."

"Yes we would!" exclaimed Hans. "It's all written down in my book."

"What does the book say?" asked his parents.

So Hans read them the old tale of "The Woodcutter and His Wife." They had had the same argument: Adam and Eve were the cause of all their misery, and they would never have been so inquisitive.

Just then, the king passed by. "Come home with me," he said. "You shall live as well as I do, with seven courses for dinner. Only don't open the tureen that's on the table; if you touch it, that will be the end of your fine living."

"I wonder what's in the tureen," said the wife.

"It's no business of ours," said the husband.

"It's not that I'm nosy," said the wife, "I'd just like to know why we may not lift the lid. It must be some delicacy."

"As long as it's not some machine," said the husband, "that will go off like a pistol and wake the whole house."

"Oh!" said the wife, and she left the tureen alone. But that night she dreamed that the lid lifted itself, and she smelled the finest punch, the kind

that you get at weddings and funerals. And there was a silver coin, with the inscription, "Drink this punch, and you will become the richest people in the world, and all the rest will be beggars." When she woke up, she told her husband about it.

"It's too much on your mind," he said.

"We could just lift the lid a little," she said. "As gently as can be."

"Very gently," said the husband.

So the wife raised the lid a fraction, and out sprang two lively little mice, and disappeared down a mousehole.

"Good night!" said the king. "Now you can go home and stew in your own juice. Don't be so critical of Adam and Eve — you've been just as inquisitive and ungrateful yourselves."

"I wonder where the book got that story from," said Ole. "It might have been us! That's given us something to think about."

The next day they went back to work. They were scorched by the sun and soaked by the rain, and they got cross and grumpy.

That evening, they brooded over their thoughts. It was still light when they had eaten their milk porridge, so Ole said, "Read us the story of the woodcutter and his wife again."

"There are lots of stories in the book," said Hans. "Stories you don't know."

"I don't care about them. I want to hear the one I know."

So Ole and Kirsten listened to the story again. Many an evening they came back to that story.

"It still doesn't explain everything," said Ole one night. "People are like milk. Some of it separates into rich curds, and some of it into watery whey. Some people have all the luck. They live like lords and never know sorrow or want."

Hans was listening. Though he was weak in the legs, he was wise in the head. So he read them another tale from his book; the one about "The Man

Who Didn't Know Sorrow or Want."

The king lay sick and could not be cured, except by wearing the shirt off the back of a man who had never known sorrow or want.

Messengers were sent far and wide to all the kings and noblemen, who should have been happy. But all of them had known sorrow and want at one time or another.

"Well, I haven't," said the swineherd, who sat laughing and singing in the ditch. "I'm the happiest man alive."

"Then give us your shirt," said the messengers. "You shall have half the kingdom for it."

But the swineherd, though he said he was the happiest man in the world, did not possess a shirt.

"That was a smart chap!" shouted Ole, and he and his wife had their best laugh in years.

The schoolmaster was passing by, and he said, "What's up? Have you won the lottery?" For the sound of laughter was not often heard from that cottage.

"Nothing like that," answered Ole. "Hans has been reading us the story of the man who didn't know sorrow or want. That man didn't even have a shirt to his back! It makes you laugh till you cry to hear something like that, especially all written down in a book. Well, we all have our troubles to bear, and knowing you're not the only one always cheers you up."

"Where did you get the book from?" asked the schoolmaster.

"Hans was given it the Christmas before last, as a present from the manor, because he's bedridden, and likes reading. At the time we would rather have had a couple of new shirts, but the book is a real eye-opener. It seems to answer your thoughts."

The schoolmaster picked up the book and opened it.

"Let's have the same story again," said Ole. "I haven't taken it all in yet. And then we can have the one about the woodcutter."

These two stories were enough for Ole. They were like two sunbeams shining into that dark cottage, and into his stunted mind, that could be so sullen and grouchy.

Hans had read the whole book time and again, for the tales took him out into the world, where his legs couldn't carry him.

The schoolmaster sat on his bed, and talked with him about it, and they both enjoyed themselves.

From then on, the schoolmaster often came to see Hans in the afternoon, while his parents were out. These visits were great fun for the boy, for the old man told him about the size of the earth, and its many lands, and how the sun was almost half a million times bigger than the earth, and so far away that it would take a cannon ball twenty-five years to reach it, though the sun's rays reach the earth in just eight minutes. Every schoolboy knew these things, but they were new to Hans, and even more wonderful than the stories in his book of fairy tales.

The schoolmaster sometimes dined at the manor, and on one visit he told the master and mistress how much the book had meant to that humble home. Two stories alone were an inspiration and a blessing. By reading them, the clever young invalid had brought laughter and food for thought into the house.

As the schoolmaster was leaving, the mistress gave him some money to give to Hans.

"That should go to my parents," said Hans, when the schoolmaster gave him the money.

And Ole and Kirsten said, "Bless him! Hans is some use after all."

A few days after that, the mistress stopped her carriage outside the cottage. She was so delighted that her Christmas present had given so much pleasure to the boy and his parents, that she had brought some more. There was fine bread, fruit, and a flask of sweet syrup, but best of all was a blackbird in a gilded cage. She put the cage on a chest of drawers not far from the boy's bed, so that he could see the bird, and listen to its lovely song. In fact, even passers-by could hear the bird singing.

Ole and Kirsten didn't get home until long after the mistress had gone. Though they could see how happy Hans was, they felt the present was just another burden. "It's just another thing for us to look after," they said, "for Hans can't do it. These rich folk, they never think things through. In the end the cat will get it."

A week passed, and then another. The cat often came into the room, but it did not harm the bird, or even frighten it. Then one afternoon, while the parents and the other children were out at work, it happened. Hans was reading his book of fairy tales. He'd got to the story about the fisherman's wife, who had all her wishes granted. She wished to be a king, and she was. She wished to be an emperor, and she was. Then she wished to be God — and ended up back in the ditch where she started.

The story didn't have any bearing on the bird and the cat. It was just the one Hans was reading at the time, and he remembered it ever after.

The cage stood on the chest of drawers; the cat sat on the floor, fixing the bird with its greeny-yellow eyes. The look seemed to say, "You look good enough to eat!"

Hans could read it in the cat's face.

"Scoot, cat!" he shouted. "Get out!" But it tensed itself for the pounce.

Hans couldn't reach it, and he had nothing to throw but his treasure, the book of fairy tales. So he threw that; but the binding had come loose, and it flew one way and pages flew the other. The cat turned round and glared at the boy, as if to say, "Don't meddle in my affairs, little Hans. I can run and jump, and you can't do either."

Hans kept his eye on the cat. He was getting worried, and so was the bird. There was no one he could call. It was as if the cat knew it. Again it got ready to leap. Hans flapped his bedcover at it, and finally hurled it across the room, but the cat took no notice. It just jumped up onto a chair, and then the

windowsill, so that it was right next to the bird.

Hans could feel his blood pounding, but he wasn't thinking of himself, he was only thinking of the cat and the bird. He couldn't get out of bed; his legs wouldn't carry him. It felt as if his heart turned over inside him, when he saw the cat spring from the windowsill to the chest of drawers, and knock the cage over. The bird was fluttering against the bars.

Hans shrieked and, without a thought of what he was doing, jumped out of bed, snatched up the cage, and shooed the cat away. With the cage in his hand he ran out of the door and into the road. Tears were streaming down his face, and he shouted at the top of his voice, "I can walk! I can walk!"

He had regained the use of his legs. Such things can happen, and it happened to him.

The schoolmaster lived nearby. The boy ran to him in his bare feet and nightshirt, carrying the bird in its cage. "I can walk!" he shouted. "Thanks be to God!" and he burst once more into tears of joy.

And there was joy at home with Ole and Kirsten. "We shall never see a happier day," they said.

Hans was called up to the manor, though he hadn't been that way for years. The trees and bushes seemed to nod to him, saying, "Hello, Hans! It's good to see you." The sun shone on his face, and in his heart.

The master and mistress were as happy as if Hans was their own son; especially the mistress, because she had given him both the book of fairy tales and the caged bird.

It is true that the bird had died — died of fright — but it had been the cause of his recovery; and the book had been an inspiration to the boy and his parents. He meant to keep it and read it always, however old he grew. And now he would be able to learn a trade — perhaps become a bookbinder, "because," he said, "then I would get all the new books to read!"

Later that day the mistress sent for Kirsten and Ole. She talked with them about Hans, who was so bright and eager, and quick to learn. "Heaven helps

26

those who help themselves."

That night Ole and Kirsten were very happy, especially Kirsten; but a week later she was crying, for dear Hans was leaving them. He was all dressed in new clothes, and he was going over the salt sea, to school. It would be years before they saw him again.

He left the book of fairy tales behind, for his parents wanted it to remember him by. Ole often read it, though only the two stories that he already knew.

Hans wrote to them of course, and each letter was happier than the last. The family he was boarding with were good to him, and school was wonderful. There was so much to learn, he wished he could live to be a hundred, and be a schoolmaster.

"If only we could live to see the day!" said his parents, and they pressed each other's hands, as solemn as if they were in church.

"What a turnabout for Hans!" said Ole. "It shows, God doesn't forget the poor man's child. Why, it's just like something Hans might have read us from his book of fairy tales!"

THE CHRISTMAS CUCKOO

FRANCES BROWNE

Once upon a time there stood in the midst of a bleak moor, in the north country, a certain village. All its inhabitants were poor, for their fields were barren and they had little trade; but the poorest of them all were two brothers called Scrub and Spare, who followed the cobbler's craft and had but one stall between them. It was a hut built of clay and wattles. The door was low and always open by day, for there was no window. The roof did not entirely keep out the rain and the only thing comfortable about it was a wide hearth, for which the brothers could never find wood enough to make a sufficient fire. There they worked in most brotherly friendship, though with little encouragement.

The people of that village were not extravagant in shoes, and better cobblers than Scrub and Spare might be found. Spiteful people said there were no shoes so bad that they would not be worse for their mending. Nevertheless Scrub and Spare managed to live between their own trade, a small barley field and a cottage garden, till one unlucky day when a new cobbler arrived in the village. He had lived in the capital city of the kingdom, and by his own account cobbled for the queen and the princesses. His awls were sharp, his lasts were new; he set up his stall in a neat cottage with two windows. The villagers soon found out that one patch of his would outwear two of the brothers'. In short, all the mending left Scrub and Spare and went to the new cobbler. The season had been wet and cold, their barley did not ripen well, and the cabbages never half closed in the garden. So the brothers were poor that winter, and when Christmas came they had nothing to feast on but a barley loaf, a piece of rusty bacon, and some small beer of their own brewing. Worse than that, the snow was very deep and they could get no firewood. Their hut stood at the end of the village and beyond it spread the bleak moor, now all white and silent; but that moor had once been a forest and great roots of old trees were still to be found in it, loosened from the soil and laid bare by the winds and rains — one of these, a rough, gnarled log, lay hard by their door, the half of it above the snow, and Spare said to his brother:

"Shall we sit here cold on Christmas while the great root lies yonder? Let us chop it up for firewood; the work will make us warm."

"No," said Scrub; "it's not right to chop wood on Christmas; besides, that root is too hard to be broken with any hatchet."

"Hard or not we must have a fire," replied Spare. "Come, brother, help me in with it. Poor as we are, there is nobody in the village will have such a yule log as ours."

Scrub liked a little grandeur, and in hopes of having a fine yule log both brothers strained and strove with all their might till, between pulling and pushing, the great old root was safe on the hearth and beginning to crackle and blaze with the red embers. In high glee the cobblers sat down to their beer and bacon. The door was shut, for there was nothing but cold moonlight and snow outside; but the hut, strewn with fir boughs, and ornamented with holly, looked cheerful as the ruddy blaze flared up and rejoiced their hearts.

"Long life and good fortune to ourselves, brother!" said Spare. "I hope you will drink that toast, and may we never have a worse fire on Christmas — but what is that?"

Spare set down the drinking-horn, and the brothers listened astonished,

29

for out of the blazing root they heard, "Cuckoo! cuckoo!" as plain as ever the spring-bird's voice came over the moor on a May morning.

"It is something bad," said Scrub, terribly frightened.

"Maybe not," said Spare, and out of the deep hole at the side which the fire had not reached flew a large grey cuckoo, and lit on the table before them. Much as the cobblers had been surprised, they were still more so when it said:

"Good gentlemen, what season is this?"

"It's Christmas," said Spare.

"Then a merry Christmas to you!" said the cuckoo. "I went to sleep in the hollow of that old root one evening last summer and never woke till the heat of your fire made me think it was summer again; but now, since you have burned my lodging, let me stay in your hut till the spring comes round — I only want a hole to sleep in, and when I go on my travels next summer be assured I will bring you some present for your trouble."

"Stay, and welcome," said Spare, while Scrub sat wondering if it were something bad or not; "I'll make you a good warm hole in the thatch. But you must be hungry after that long sleep. Here is a slice of barley bread. Come, help us to keep Christmas!"

The cuckoo ate up the slice, drank water from the brown jug, for he would take no beer, and flew into a snug hole which Spare scooped for him in the thatch of the hut.

Scrub said he was afraid it wouldn't be lucky; but as it slept on and the days passed he forgot his fears. So the snow melted, the heavy rains came, the cold grew less, the days lengthened, and one sunny morning the brothers were awakened by the cuckoo shouting its own cry to let them know the spring had come.

"Now I'm going on my travels," said the bird, "over the world to tell men of the spring. There is no country where trees bud or flowers bloom that I will not cry in before the year goes round. Give me another slice of barley

30

bread to keep me on my journey and tell me what present I shall bring you at the twelvemonth's end."

Scrub would have been angry with his brother for cutting so large a slice, their store of barley-meal being low; but his mind was occupied with what present would be most prudent to ask; at length a lucky thought struck him.

"Good master cuckoo," said he, "if a great traveller who sees all the world like you, could know of any place where diamonds or pearls were to be found, one of a tolerable size brought in your beak would help such poor men as my brother and I to provide something better than barley bread for your next entertainment."

"I know nothing of diamonds or pearls," said the cuckoo; "they are in the hearts of rocks and the sands of rivers. My knowledge is only of that which grows on the earth. But there are two trees hard by the well that lies at the world's end: one of them is called the golden tree, for its leaves are all of beaten gold; every winter they fall into the well with a sound like scattered coin, and I know not what becomes of them. As for the other, it is always green like a laurel. Some call it the wise, and some the merry tree. Its leaves never fall, but they that get one of them keep a blithe heart in spite of all misfortunes and can make themselves as merry in a hut as in a palace."

"Good master cuckoo, bring me a leaf off that tree!" cried Spare.

"Now, brother, don't be a fool!" said Scrub. "Think of the leaves of beaten gold! Dear master cuckoo, bring me one of them!"

Before another word could be spoken, the cuckoo had flown out of the open door, and was shouting its spring cry over moor and meadow. The brothers were poorer than ever that year; nobody would send them a single shoe to mend. The new cobbler said in scorn they should come to be his apprentices; and Scrub and Spare would have left the village but for their barley-field, their cabbage garden and a certain maid called Fairfeather, whom both the cobblers had courted for seven years without even knowing which she meant to favour.

Sometimes Fairfeather seemed inclined to Scrub, sometimes she smiled on Spare; but the brothers never disputed for that. They sowed their barley, planted their cabbage and, now that their trade was gone, worked in the rich villagers' fields to make out a scanty living. So the seasons came and passed: spring, summer, harvest and winter followed each other as they have done from the beginning. At the end of the last, Scrub and Spare had grown so poor and ragged that Fairfeather thought them beneath her notice. Old neighbours forgot to invite them to wedding feasts or merrymaking; and they thought the cuckoo had forgotten them too, when at daybreak, on the first of April, they heard a hard beak knocking at their door and a voice crying:

"Cuckoo! cuckoo! Let me in with my presents."

Spare ran to open the door, and in came the cuckoo, carrying on one side of his bill a golden leaf larger than that of any tree in the north country; and in the other, one like that of the common laurel, only it had a fresher green.

"Here," it said, giving the gold to Scrub and the green to Spare, "it is a long carriage from the world's end. Give me a slice of barley bread, for I must tell the north country that the spring has come."

Scrub did not grudge the thickness of that slice, though it was cut from their last loaf. So much gold had never been in the cobbler's hands before and he could not help exulting over his brother.

"See the wisdom of my choice!" he said, holding up the large leaf of gold. "As for yours, as good might be plucked from any hedge. I wonder a sensible bird would carry the like so far."

"Good master cobbler," cried the cuckoo, finishing the slice, "your conclusions are more hasty than courteous. If your brother be disappointed this time, I go on the same journey every year, and for your hospitable entertainment will think it no trouble to bring each of you whichever leaf you desire."

"Darling cuckoo," cried Scrub, "bring me a golden one"; and Spare, looking up from the green leaf on which he gazed as though it were a crown jewel, said:

"Be sure to bring me one from the merry tree," and away flew the cuckoo.

"This is the Feast of All Fools, and it ought to be your birthday," said Scrub. "Did ever man fling away such an opportunity of getting rich! Much good your merry leaves will do in the midst of rags and poverty!" So he went on, but Spare laughed at him and answered with quaint old proverbs concerning the cares that come with gold, till Scrub, at length getting angry, vowed his brother was not fit to live with a respectable man; and taking his lasts, his awls and his golden leaf, he left the wattle hut and went to tell the villagers.

They were astonished at the folly of Spare and charmed with Scrub's good sense, particularly when he showed them the golden leaf, and told that the cuckoo would bring him one every spring. The new cobbler immediately took him into partnership, the greatest people sent him their shoes to mend, Fairfeather smiled graciously upon him and in the course of that summer they were married, with a grand wedding feast, at which the whole village danced, except Spare, who was not invited, because the bride could not bear his low-mindedness, and his brother thought him a disgrace to the family.

Indeed all who heard the story concluded that Spare must be mad, and nobody would associate with him but a lame tinker, a beggar-boy and a poor woman reputed to be a witch because she was old and ugly. As for Scrub, he established himself with Fairfeather in a cottage close by that of the new cobbler, and quite as fine. There he mended shoes to everybody's satisfaction, had a scarlet coat for holidays and a fat goose for dinner every wedding-day. Fairfeather too had a crimson gown and fine blue ribands; but neither she nor Scrub were content, for to buy this grandeur the golden leaf had to be broken and parted with piece by piece, so the last morsel was gone before the cuckoo came with another.

Spare lived on in the old hut, and worked in the cabbage garden. (Scrub had got the barley-field because he was the elder.) Every day his coat grew more ragged, and the hut more weatherbeaten; but people remarked that he never looked sad nor sour; and the wonder was that, from the time they began to keep his company, the tinker grew kinder to the poor ass with which he travelled the country, the beggar-boy kept out of mischief and the old woman was never cross to her cat or angry with the children.

Every first of April the cuckoo came tapping at their doors with the golden leaf to Scrub and the green to Spare. Fairfeather would have entertained him nobly with wheaten bread and honey, for she had some notion of persuading him to bring two gold leaves instead of one, but the cuckoo flew away to eat barley bread with Spare, saying he was not fit company for fine people, and liked the old hut where he slept so snugly from Christmas till spring.

Scrub spent the golden leaves, and Spare kept the merry ones; and I know not how many years passed in this manner, when a certain great lord who owned that village came to the neighbourhood. His castle stood on the moor. It was ancient and strong, with high towers and a deep moat. All the country, as far as one could see from the highest turret, belonged to its lord; but he had not been there for twenty years, and would not have come then, only he was melancholy. The cause of his grief was that he had been prime minister at court and in high favour, till somebody told the crown prince that he had spoken disrespectfully concerning the turning out of his royal highness's toes, and said of the king that he did not lay on taxes enough, whereon the north country lord was turned out of office and banished to his own estate. There he lived for some weeks in very bad temper. The servants said nothing would please him, and the villagers put on their worst clothes lest he should raise their rents; but one day in the harvest time his lordship chanced to meet Spare gathering watercresses at a meadow stream, and fell into talk with the cobbler.

How it was nobody could tell, but from the hour of that discourse the great lord cast away his melancholy: he forgot his lost office and his court enemies, the king's taxes and the crown prince's toes, and went about with a noble train, hunting, fishing and making merry in his hall, where all travellers were entertained and all the poor were welcome. This strange story spread through the north country, and great company came to the cobbler's hut — rich men who had lost their money, poor men who had lost their friends, beauties who had grown old, wits who had gone out of fashion — all came to talk with Spare, and whatever their troubles had been, all went home merry. The rich gave him presents, the poor gave him thanks. Spare's coat ceased to be ragged, he had bacon with his cabbage and the villagers began to think there was some sense in him.

By this time his fame had reached the capital city, and even the court. There were a great many discontented people there besides the king, who had lately fallen into ill humour because a neighbouring princess, with seven islands for her dowry, would not marry his eldest son. So a royal messenger was sent to Spare, with a velvet mantle, a diamond ring and a command that he should repair to court immediately.

"Tomorrow is the first of April," said Spare, "and I will go with you two hours after sunrise."

The messenger lodged all night at the castle, and the cuckoo came at sunrise with the merry leaf.

"Court is a fine place," he said when the cobbler told him he was going, "but I cannot come there, they would lay snares and catch me; so be careful of the leaves I have brought you, and give me a farewell slice of barley bread."

Spare was sorry to part with the cuckoo, little as he had of his company; but he gave him a slice which would have broken Scrub's heart in former times, it was so thick and large; and having sewed up the leaves in the lining of his leather doublet, he set out with the messenger on his way to court.

His coming caused great surprise there. Everybody wondered what the king could see in such a common-looking man; but scarce had his majesty conversed with him half an hour, when the princess and her seven islands were forgotten, and orders given that a feast for all comers should be spread in the banquet hall. The princes of the blood, the great lords and ladies, ministers of state and judges of the land, after that, discoursed with Spare, and the more they talked the lighter grew their hearts, so that such changes had never been seen at court. The lords forgot their spites and the ladies their envies, the princes and ministers made friends among themselves, and the judges showed no favour.

As for Spare, he had a chamber assigned him in the palace and a seat at the king's table; one sent him rich robes and another costly jewels; but in the midst of all his grandeur he still wore the leathern doublet, which the palace servants thought remarkably mean. One day the king's attention being drawn to it by the chief page, his majesty inquired why Spare didn't give it to a beggar? But the cobbler answered:

"High and mighty monarch, this doublet was with me before silk and velvet came — I find it easier to wear than the court cut; moreover it serves to keep me humble, by recalling the days when it was my holiday garment."

The king thought this a wise speech, and commanded that no one should find fault with the leathern doublet. So things went, till tidings of his brother's good fortune reached Scrub in the moorland cottage on another first of April, when the cuckoo came with two golden leaves, because he had none to carry for Spare.

"Think of that!" said Fairfeather. "Here we are spending our lives in this humdrum place, and Spare making his fortune at court with two or three paltry green leaves! What would they say to our golden ones? Let us pack up and make our way to the king's palace; I'm sure he will make you a lord and me a lady of honour, not to speak of all the fine clothes and presents we shall have."

Scrub thought this excellent reasoning, and their packing up began; but it was soon found that the cottage contained few things fit for carrying to court. Fairfeather could not think of her wooden bowls, spoons and trenchers being seen there. Scrub considered his lasts and awls better left behind, as without them, he concluded, no one would suspect him of being a cobbler. So putting on their holiday clothes, Fairfeather took her looking-glass and Scrub his drinking-horn, which happened to have a very thin rim of silver, and each carrying a golden leaf carefully wrapped up that none might see it till they reached the palace, the pair set out in great expectation.

How far Scrub and Fairfeather journeyed I cannot say, but when the sun was high and warm at noon, they came into a wood both tired and hungry.

"If I had known it was so far to court," said Scrub, "I would have brought the end of that barley loaf which we left in the cupboard."

"Husband," said Fairfeather, "you shouldn't have such mean thoughts: how could one eat barley bread on the way to a palace? Let us rest ourselves under this tree, and look at our golden leaves to see if they are safe." In looking at the leaves, and talking of their fine prospects, Scrub and Fairfeather did not perceive that a very thin old woman had slipped from behind the tree, with a long staff in her hand and a great wallet by her side.

"Noble lord and lady," she said, "for I know you are such by your voices, though my eyes are dim and my hearing none of the sharpest, will you condescend to tell me where I may find some water to mix a bottle of mead which I carry in my wallet, because it is too strong for me?"

As the old woman spoke, she pulled out a large wooden bottle such as shepherds used in the ancient times, corked with leaves rolled together and having a small wooden cup hanging from its handle.

"Perhaps you will do me the favour to taste," she said. "It is only made of the best honey. I have also cream cheese and a wheaten loaf here, if such honourable persons as you would eat the like."

Scrub and Fairfeather became very condescending after this speech. They were now sure that there must be some appearance of nobility about them; besides, they were very hungry, and having hastily wrapped up the golden leaves, they assured the old woman they were not at all proud, notwithstanding the lands and castles they had left behind them in the north country, and would willingly help to lighten the wallet. The old woman could scarcely be persuaded to sit down for pure humility, but at length she did, and before the wallet was half empty Scrub and Fairfeather firmly believed that there must be something remarkably noble-looking about them. This was not entirely owing to her ingenious discourse. The old woman was a wood-witch; her name was Buttertongue; and all her time was spent in making mead, which, being boiled with curious herbs and spells, had the power of making all who drank it fall asleep and dream with their eyes open. She had two dwarfs of sons; one was named Spy and the other Pounce. Wherever their mother went they were not far behind; and whoever tasted her mead was sure to be robbed by the dwarfs.

Scrub and Fairfeather sat leaning against the old tree. The cobbler had a lump of cheese in his hand; his wife held fast a hunch of bread. Their eyes and mouths were both open, but they were dreaming of great grandeur at court, when the old woman raised her shrill voice:

"What ho, my sons, come here and carry home the harvest!"

No sooner had she spoken than the two little dwarfs darted out of the neighbouring thicket.

"Idle boys!" cried the mother. "What have you done today to help our living?"

"I have been to the city," said Spy, "and could see nothing. These are hard times for us — everybody minds his business so contentedly since that cobbler came; but here is a leathern doublet which his page threw out of the window; it's of no use, but I brought it to let you see I was not idle." And he tossed down Spare's doublet, with the merry leaves in it, which he had carried like a bundle on his little back.

To explain how Spy came by it, I must tell you that the forest was not far from the great city where Spare lived in such high esteem. All things had gone well with the cobbler till the king thought it was quite unbecoming to see such a worthy man without a servant. His majesty, therefore, to let all men understand his royal favour towards Spare, appointed one of his own pages to wait upon him. The name of this youth was Tinseltoes, and though he was the seventh of the king's pages nobody in all the court had grander notions. Nothing could please him that had not gold or silver about it, and his grandmother feared he would hang himself for being appointed page to a cobbler. As for Spare, if anything could have troubled him, this token of his majesty's kindness would have done it.

The honest man had been so used to serve himself that the page was always in the way, but his merry leaves came to his assistance; and, to the great surprise of his grandmother, Tinseltoes took wonderfully to the new service. Some said it was because Spare gave him nothing to do but play at bowls all day on the palace green. Yet one thing grieved the heart of Tinseltoes, and that was his master's leathern doublet; but for it, he was persuaded, people would never remember that Spare had been a cobbler, and the page took a deal of pains to let him see how unfashionable it was at court; but Spare answered Tinseltoes as he had done the king, and at last, finding nothing better would do, the page got up one fine morning earlier than his master, and tossed the leathern doublet out of the back window into a certain lane where Spy found it, and brought it to his mother.

"That nasty thing!" said the old woman. "Where is the good in it?"

By this time Pounce had taken everything of value from Scrub and Fairfeather — the looking-glass, the silver-rimmed horn, the husband's scarlet coat, the wife's gay mantle, and above all the golden leaves, which so rejoiced old Butter-tongue and her sons that they threw the leathern doublet over the sleeping cobbler for a jest, and went off to their hut in the heart of the forest.

The sun was going down when Scrub and Fairfeather awoke from dreaming that they had been made a lord and a lady and sat clothed in silk and velvet, feasting with the king in his palace hall. It was a great disappointment to find their golden leaves and all their best things gone. Scrub tore his hair and vowed to take the old woman's life, while Fairfeather lamented sore; but Scrub, feeling cold for want of his coat, put on the leathern doublet without asking or caring whence it came.

Scarcely was it buttoned on when a change came over him; he addressed such merry discourse to Fairfeather, that, instead of lamentations, she made the wood ring with laughter. Both busied themselves in getting up a hut of boughs, in which Scrub kindled a fire with a flint and steel, which, together with his pipe, he had brought unknown to Fairfeather, who had told him the like was never heard of at court. Then they found a pheasant's nest at the root of an old oak, made a meal of roasted eggs, and went to sleep on a heap of long green grass which they had gathered, with nightingales singing all night long in the old trees about them. So it happened that Scrub and Fairfeather stayed day after day in the forest, making their hut larger and more comfortable against the winter, living on wild birds' eggs and berries and never thinking of their lost golden leaves, or their journey to court.

In the meantime Spare had got up and missed his doublet. Tinseltoes, of course, said he knew nothing about it. The whole palace was searched, and every servant questioned, till all the court wondered why such a fuss was made about an old leathern doublet. That very day things came back to their old fashion. Quarrels began among the lords and jealousies among the ladies. The king said his subjects did not pay him half enough taxes, the queen wanted more jewels, the servants took to their old bickerings and got up some new ones. Spare found himself getting wonderfully dull, and very much out of place: nobles began to ask what business a cobbler had at the king's table, and his majesty ordered the palace chronicles to be searched for a precedent. The cobbler was too wise to tell all he had lost with that doublet, but being by this time somewhat familiar with court customs, he proclaimed a reward of fifty gold pieces to any who would bring him news concerning it.

Scarcely was this made known in the city when the gates and outer courts of the palace were filled by men, women and children, some bringing leathern doublets of every cut and colour — some with tales of what they had heard and seen in their walks about the neighbourhood. And so much news concerning all sorts of great people came out of these stories that lords and ladies ran to the king with complaints of Spare as a speaker of slander; and his majesty, being now satisfied that there was no example in all the palace records of such a retainer, issued a decree banishing the cobbler for ever from court and confiscating all his goods in favour of Tinseltoes.

That royal edict was scarcely published before the page was in full possession of his rich chamber, his costly garments and all the presents the courtiers had given him; while Spare, having no longer the fifty pieces of gold to give, was glad to make his escape out of the back window, for fear of the nobles, who vowed to be revenged on him, and the crowd, who were prepared to stone him for cheating them about his doublet.

The window from which Spare let himself down with a strong rope was that from which Tinseltoes had tossed the doublet, and as the cobbler came down late in the twilight, a poor woodman with a heavy load of faggots stopped and stared at him in great astonishment.

"What's the matter, friend?" said Spare. "Did you never see a man coming down from a back window before?"

"Why," said the woodman, "the last morning I passed here a leathern doublet came out of that very window, and I'll be bound you are the owner of it."

"That I am, friend," said the cobbler. "Can you tell me which way that doublet went?"

"As I walked on," said the woodman, "a dwarf, called Spy, bundled it up and ran off to his mother in the forest."

"Honest friend," said Spare, taking off the last of his fine clothes (a grass-green mantle edged with gold), "I'll give you this if you will follow the dwarf and bring me back my doublet."

"It would not be good to carry faggots in," said the woodman. "But if you want back your doublet, the road to the forest lies at the end of this lane," and he trudged away.

Determined to find his doublet, and sure that neither crowd nor courtiers could catch him in the forest, Spare went on his way, and was soon among the tall trees; but neither hut nor dwarf could he see. Moreover the night came on; the wood was dark and tangled, but here and there the moon shone through its alleys, the great owls flitted about, and the nightingales sang. So he went on, hoping to find some place of shelter. At last the red light of a fire, gleaming through a thicket, led him to the door of a low hut. It stood half open, as if there was nothing to fear, and within he saw his brother Scrub snoring loudly on a bed of grass, at the foot of which lay his own leathern doublet; while Fairfeather, in a kirtle made of plaited rushes, sat roasting pheasants' eggs by the fire.

"Good evening, mistress," said Spare, stepping in.

The blaze shone on him, but so changed was her brother-in-law with his court life, that Fairfeather did not know him, and she answered far more courteously than was her wont.

"Good evening, master. Whence come ye so late? But speak low, for my good man has sorely tired himself cleaving wood, and is taking a sleep, as you see, before supper."

"A good rest to him," said Spare, perceiving he was not known. "I come from the court for a day's hunting, and have lost my way in the forest."

"Sit down and have a share of our supper," said Fairfeather. "I will put some more eggs in the ashes; and tell me the news of court — I used to think of it long ago when I was young and foolish."

"Did you never go there?" said the cobbler, "So fair a dame as you would

make the ladies marvel."

"You are pleased to flatter," said Fairfeather; "but my husband has a brother there, and we left our moorland village to try our fortune also. An old woman enticed us with fair words and strong drink at the entrance of this forest, where we fell asleep and dreamt of great things; but when we woke, everything had been robbed from us — my looking-glass, my scarlet cloak, my husband's Sunday coat; and, in place of all, the robbers left him that old leathern doublet, which he has worn ever since, and never was so merry in all his life, though we live in this poor hut."

"It is a shabby doublet, that," said Spare, taking up the garment, and seeing that it was his own, for the merry leaves were still sewed in its lining. "It would be good for hunting in, however — your husband would be glad to part with it, I dare say, in exchange for this handsome cloak"; and he pulled off the green mantle and buttoned on the doublet, much to Fairfeather's delight, who ran and shook Scrub, crying:

"Husband! husband! rise and see what a good bargain I have made!"

Scrub gave one closing snore, and muttered something about the root being hard; but he rubbed his eyes, gazed up at his brother, and said:

"Spare, is that really you? How did you like the court, and have you made your fortune?"

"That I have, brother," said Spare, "in getting back my own good leathern doublet. Come, let us eat eggs and rest ourselves here this night. In the morning we will return to our own old hut, at the end of the moorland village where the Christmas Cuckoo will come and bring us leaves."

Scrub and Fairfeather agreed. So in the morning they all returned, and found the old hut the worse for wear and weather. The neighbours came about them to ask the news of court, and see if they had made their fortune. Everybody was astonished to find the three poorer than ever, but somehow they liked to go back to the hut. Spare brought out the lasts and awls he had hidden in a corner; Scrub and he began their old trade, and the whole north country found out that there never were such cobblers.

They mended the shoes of lords and ladies as well as the common people; everybody was satisfied. Their custom increased from day to day, and all that were disappointed, discontented or unlucky came to the hut as in old times before Spare went to court.

The rich brought them presents, the poor did them service. The hut itself changed, no one knew how. Flowering honeysuckle grew over its roof; red and white roses grew thick about its door. Moreover the Christmas Cuckoo always came on the first of April, bringing three leaves of the merry tree — for Scrub and Fairfeather would have no more golden ones. So it was with them when I last heard the news of the north country.

THE NUTCRACKER

E.T.A. HOFFMANN

Retold by Neil Philip

It was Christmas Eve. All day, little Marie and her brother Fritz had been waiting for the evening, when they would receive their Christmas presents. All day, they had been listening to banging and crashing from behind the locked door where Godfather Drosselmeier had been busy making a special present for them; but they had no idea what it would be. Every year, Godfather Drosselmeier, the clockmaker, made them something wonderful.

When dark came, Mother and Father led them to the tree, that sparkled with hundreds of candles, and was hung with presents of all kinds — dolls, and toy soldiers, nuts, and sweets. Then it was time for Godfather Drosselmeier's present. It was splendid, and so clever. It was a castle on a beautiful lawn, with people inside who moved by clockwork, and one, who looked just like Godfather Drosselmeier himself, who came right out of the house to stand by the gate, and then went back in again.

But, sad to say, Fritz and Marie were so excited by their other presents, they scarcely had time to appreciate how wonderful it was. They watched it for a while, and then Fritz said, "Doesn't it do anything else?"

"No, I'm afraid not," said Godfather Drosselmeier, and that was that. Mother and Father could see that he was hurt, so they made a big point of asking him to show them the whole thing again, and that cheered him up a bit.

Marie didn't notice, for she had found something really fascinating under the tree. It was a wooden figure of a soldier, a hussar, very smart and standing to attention. Funnily enough, he looked a bit like Godfather Drosselmeier, with his big jaw and kind face.

Fritz said, "He's a Nutcracker! You put a nut between his teeth, and he bites it open." So Marie put in a nut.

Crack! Out fell the nut, ready to eat.

Marie was delighted with her new friend, the Nutcracker. But Fritz said, "Give him to me. I want a go." Then Fritz found the hardest, biggest nut, and put it in the Nutcracker's mouth.

There was a terrible splintering sound. The nut had broken the Nutcracker's jaw.

"What a useless Nutcracker!" said Fritz. But Marie picked it up, and cradled it in her arms, and dressed its hurt jaw with her handkerchief.

That night, when everyone had gone to bed, Marie got up to see if the Nutcracker was all right. As she picked it up, the clock struck midnight.

Suddenly, the room was full of mice — a whole army of them. And at their head was the Mouse King, a terrible sight with his seven heads and his cruel cutlass. They were advancing on the toy cupboard. Fritz's soldiers, his pride and joy, and Marie's beloved dolls, were under siege!

Then the Nutcracker seemed to wake up. Green sparks seemed to shoot from his eyes. "Toys!" he shouted, "Follow me, to glory!"

Then there was a terrible fight between the toys and the mice. The toys were brave, but they were so few, and the mice were so many. At last, the Nutcracker was brought down, and the Mouse King charged him, squealing his battle cry from seven throbbing throats.

Marie thought she would faint from terror. But she couldn't abandon the Nutcracker to his fate. She took off her left shoe and threw it, as hard as she could, at the Mouse King. Then she fainted away, crashing into the glass-fronted toy cupboard as she fell to the floor.

The next thing Marie knew, she was lying in her bed, with a bandaged arm where she had cut herself on the broken glass, and a face as pale as a doll's. Mother was sitting by her side, and the doctor was standing at the foot of the bed.

"What's happened to the Nutcracker?" asked Marie. "Did the Mouse King get him?"

"Hush now," said Mother. "You've had a bad dream. Just rest."

But Marie kept asking and asking about the Nutcracker, so finally Mother said, "The Nutcracker is safe in the toy cupboard. Don't fret, darling. The Nutcracker is safe." So Marie went to sleep happy, and began to get better from that moment, though all her dreams were full of the Nutcracker.

She woke from one of those dreams, and there was Godfather Drosselmeier, standing by her bed, holding the Nutcracker in his hands. He had mended the hurt jaw, and the Nutcracker looked as smart as ever.

Marie tried to tell Godfather Drosselmeier all about the Nutcracker and the Mouse King.

Then he said, "You have told me a story, so I shall tell you one. It is called the Tale of the Hard Nut."

This is the story he told.

Once there were a king and queen, and they had a baby daughter named Pirlipat, and of course she was a princess — the most beautiful little princess there ever was.

When she was born, everyone was so happy. But the queen seemed very worried about the baby, and insisted that she must be guarded by six nursemaids all through the night, and that each of those six nurses should have a purring tomcat on her lap all that time. They had to keep stroking the cats to make sure that they kept purring. No one knew why.

This is the reason. A few months before, the queen had been making sausages in the kitchen, because she was the only one who could cook them just as the king liked them. When the sausage mixture was sizzling in the pan, the queen heard a tiny voice, piping, "Give me some fat, sister, for I am a queen too, and I am hungry." It was Madam Mousie, the queen of the mice. So the queen gave her some fat.

Then Madam Mousie's seven sons came out, and gobbled up all the rest of the fat, so there was none for the king's sausages.

The poor queen didn't know what to do. When she served the sausages to the king, the poor man turned quite pale. "Whatever's wrong, dear heart?" she asked.

"Not enough fat," he replied.

So it all came out about Madam Mousie and her seven sons. The king was furious. He called for the court clockmaker, whose name just happened to be Drosselmeier, and ordered him to rid the palace of all mice. And Drosselmeier made a mousetrap, and caught all seven of Madam Mousie's greedy sons. But Madam Mousie was too clever to be caught in any trap.

Instead, the queen of the mice hissed up at the human queen, when next she was making sausages, "My seven sons are dead. Be careful I don't come when your baby is born, and bite it in two!"

So that was why the queen was so worried, and why Princess Pirlipat was guarded all night by six nursemaids with six purring tomcats.

Now one night, the six nursemaids all fell asleep. They stopped stroking the tomcats, and the tomcats stopped purring. That was when Madam Mousie struck.

One of the nursemaids woke up just in time, and screamed, and saved the princess from being bitten in two — but it was too late to stop Madam Mousie putting a spell on the poor girl. From being the most beautiful baby in the world, Pirlipat had turned into the ugliest.

The king blamed Drosselmeier, the court clockmaker, for the disaster, because he had not managed to catch Madam Mousie in his mousetrap. "You must find out how to free the princess from this terrible spell," he said. "Otherwise, I will have your head cut off!"

So Drosselmeier searched everywhere for a cure for the princess, and eventually he discovered that she could only be cured by eating the Crackatuck nut. The Crackatuck nut was a nut so hard that it could only be cracked between the teeth of a young man who had never shaved, and never worn boots, and he must give the princess the nut with his eyes closed, and then take seven steps backwards without stumbling before he opened them again.

Drosselmeier told the king this, and the king said, "In that case, Drosselmeier, all you need to do is find the nut, and a young man to crack it open, and you can keep your head. And what's more, the young man can have my daughter's hand in marriage, and my kingdom, too."

The poor clockmaker went all over the kingdom looking for the Crackatuck nut. Finally, after years of searching, he discovered that the nut belonged to his own cousin, a dollmaker. And what's more, the dollmaker's son, young Drosselmeier, had never shaved and never worn boots.

They went back to the court, and young Drosselmeier cracked the Crackatuck nut between his teeth, and presented it to Princess Pirlipat with his eyes closed. As soon as the princess — who was by now quite grown up — ate the nut, she became beautiful again.

The whole court cheered and shouted. But young Drosselmeier was still taking his seven steps backwards. At the last moment, Madam Mousie ran out and tripped him, and he fell sprawling to the floor, where he turned from a handsome young man into a funny old Nutcracker.

He had trodden on Madam Mousie, and broken her neck. But with her dying breath she said, "My seven-headed son will be Mouse King now, and he will avenge me, Nutcracker!" And then she died.

The king was still willing to keep his word, but when Princess Pirlipat saw the Nutcracker she said, "Take that ugly thing away!"

Drosselmeier the clockmaker was very sad that his nephew, young Drosselmeier, had been turned into a Nutcracker, and wasn't after all going to marry the princess and rule the kingdom. He consulted all the wise men of the land, and they all said that the only way to break the spell was for young Drosselmeier to kill the seven-headed Mouse King — and find a girl to love him in spite of his ugliness.

And that was the Tale of the Hard Nut.

When Godfather Drosselmeier had left, Marie thought long and hard about this tale, and she began to see that it was the story behind the dreadful fight she had witnessed between the Nutcracker and the Mouse King. The court clockmaker was none other than Godfather Drosselmeier himself, and the Nutcracker was his enchanted nephew, young Drosselmeier.

That night, Marie woke up in the moonlight to find the seven-headed Mouse King crouching on the table by her bed. "Give me your candy and your marzipan," the Mouse King hissed, "or I'll bite your Nutcracker in two."

Marie was so frightened for the poor Nutcracker. In the evening she put all her candy in a pile in front of the toy cupboard, and that night the mice came and ate it all up.

But that wasn't the end of it. Next night the Mouse King came again. "Give me your sugar dolls, or I'll bite your Nutcracker in two."

Marie didn't know what to do. In the morning she picked up the Nutcracker and told it all her worries. "What can I do?" she asked. "Even if I give the Mouse King all my sugar dolls, he'll just come back to ask for something else. How can I protect you?"

"Find me a sword," said the Nutcracker, "and I can look after myself."

Marie was surprised to find that the Nutcracker could speak; but after all, he was a man under a spell, not just a wooden toy. She ran to her brother Fritz and begged him to lend her a sword from one of his toy soldiers, and then she buckled the sword onto the Nutcracker.

That night Marie thought she would never get to sleep. But she must have done, because she woke with a start at midnight. She heard her bedroom door creak. Was it the awful seven-headed Mouse King, come to bite her in two?

No, it was the Nutcracker. He bowed low. "My lady," he said, "have no fear. The Mouse King is dead, and will trouble you no more." And then the Nutcracker gave Marie the seven crowns from the Mouse King's heads, to show that what he said was true.

"Now," said the Nutcracker, "to show my gratitude for all that you have done for me, I would like you to come with me to my country."

Marie followed the Nutcracker downstairs into the hall. There, coming out of the sleeve of Father's coat, was a little wooden staircase. They climbed it, and it took them to the land of Sugarplums, where everything is made of candy. The rivers are made of lemonade, the villages are made of gingerbread, the towns are made of barleysugar, and the capital city is made of marzipan.

In the marzipan castle, the Nutcracker introduced Marie to his four sisters, every one a princess, for here the Nutcracker himself was a prince. The princesses were so happy to see their brother home, and so grateful to Marie for helping him. They sat down to listen to the whole story.

While the Nutcracker told his tale, his sisters busied themselves preparing a meal. Marie watched them pounding spices, squeezing fruit, and sugaring almonds, and longed to help. As if they could read her mind, the sisters gave her a little golden mortar, and asked her to crush some candy for them.

Marie was very happy pounding the candy, but, as she worked, she felt the world going misty. She seemed to be rising, rising, rising in the air, higher, and higher, till...

Plop! She landed back in bed.

Mother was standing at the door, come to check that Marie was all right. "Mother, Mother," said Marie, "you wouldn't believe where I've just been!"

And it was true: Mother didn't believe it. "You and your stories," she said.

That morning, Marie went down to see the Nutcracker, who was standing as wooden and stiff as anything. "Oh, Nutcracker," she said, "thank you for taking me to see your country. How I wish you could be freed from the spell, and be yourself again. I'm sure I wouldn't reject you, like that stuck-up Princess Pirlipat." And she threw her arms around his neck.

As she did so, the Nutcracker became warm, and grew, until instead of a wooden nutcracker, Marie was embracing a handsome young man. It was young Drosselmeier, freed from the spell, because he had killed the seven-headed Mouse King, and found a girl to love him despite his ugliness.

So Marie married young Drosselmeier, the Nutcracker Prince, and went to live with him in the marzipan castle, in the land of Sugarplums. And for all I know, they are living there still.

FATHER CHRISTMAS
AND THE CARPENTER

ALF PRØYSEN

There was once a carpenter called Anderson. He was a good father and he had a lot of children.

One Christmas Eve, while his wife and children were decorating the Christmas tree, Anderson crept out to his wood-shed. He had a surprise for them all; he was going to dress up as Father Christmas, load a sack of presents on to his sledge and go and knock on the front door. But as he pulled the loaded sledge out of the wood-shed, he slipped and fell across the sack of presents. This set the sledge moving, because the ground sloped from the sledge down to the road, and Anderson had no time even to shout "Way there!" before he crashed into another sledge which was coming down the road.

"I'm very sorry," said Anderson.

"Don't mention it; I couldn't stop myself," said the other man. Like Anderson, he was dressed in Father Christmas clothes and had a sack on his sledge.

"We seem to have the same idea," said Anderson. "I see you're all dressed up like me." He laughed and shook the other man by the hand. "My name is Anderson."

58

"Glad to meet you," said the other. "I'm Father Christmas."

"Ha, ha!" laughed Anderson. "You will have your little joke, and quite right too on Christmas Eve."

"That's what I thought," said the other man, "and if you will agree we can change places tonight, and that will be a better joke still; I'll take the presents along to *your* children if you'll go and visit *mine*. But you must take off that costume."

Anderson looked a bit puzzled. "What am I to dress up in then?"

"You don't need to dress up at all," said the other. "My children see Father Christmas all the year round, but they've never seen a real carpenter. I told them last Christmas that if they were good this year I'd try and get a carpenter to come and see them while I went round with presents for human children."

"So he really *is* Father Christmas," thought Anderson to himself. Out loud he said, "All right, if you really want me to, I will. The only thing is, I haven't any presents for your children."

"Presents?" said Father Christmas. "Aren't you a carpenter?"

"Yes, of course."

"Well, then, all you have to do is to take along a few pieces of wood, and some nails. You have a knife, I suppose?" Anderson said he had and went to look for the things in his workshop.

"Just follow my footsteps in the snow; they'll lead you to my house in the forest," said Father Christmas. "Then I'll take your sack and sledge and go and knock on your door."

"Righto!" said the carpenter.

Then Father Christmas went to knock on Anderson's door, and the carpenter trudged through the snow in Father Christmas's footsteps. They led him into the forest, past two pine-trees, a large boulder and a tree-stump. There peeping out from behind the stump were three little faces with red caps on.

"He's here! He's here!" shouted the Christmas children as they scampered in front of him to a fallen tree, lying with its roots in the air. When Anderson followed them round to the other side of the roots he found Mother Christmas standing there waiting for him.

"Here he is, Mother! He's the carpenter Dad promised us! Look at him! Isn't he tall?" The children were all shouting at once.

"Now, now, children," said Mother Christmas. "Anybody would think you'd never seen a human being before."

"We've never seen a proper *carpenter* before!" shouted the children. "Come on in, Mr. Carpenter!"

Pulling a branch aside, Mother Christmas led the way into the house. Anderson had to bend his long back double and crawl on his hands and knees. But once in, he found he could straighten up. The room had a mud floor, but it was very snug, with tree stumps for chairs, and beds made of moss with covers of plaited grass. In the smallest bed lay the Christmas baby and in the far corner sat a very old Grandfather Christmas, his red cap nodding up and down.

"Have you got a knife? Did you bring some wood and some nails?" The children pulled at Anderson's sleeve and wanted to know everything at once.

"Now, children," said Mother Christmas, "let the carpenter sit down before you start pestering him."

"Has anyone come to see me?" croaked old Grandfather Christmas.

Mother Christmas shouted in his ear, "It's Anderson, the carpenter!" She explained that Grandfather was so old he never went out any more. "He'd be pleased if you would come over and shake hands with him."

So Anderson took the old man's hand which was as hard as a piece of bark.

"Come and sit here, Mr Carpenter!" called the children.

The eldest one spoke first. "Do you know what I want you to make for me? A toboggan. Can you do that — a little one, I mean?"

"I'll try," said Anderson, and it didn't take long before he had a smart toboggan just ready to fly over the snow.

"Now it's my turn," said the little girl who had pigtails sticking straight out from her head. "I want a doll's bed."

"Have you any dolls?" asked Anderson.

"No, but I borrow the field mice sometimes, and I can play with baby squirrels as much as I like. They love being dolls. Please make me a doll's bed."

So the carpenter made her a doll's bed. Then he asked the smaller boy what he would like. But he was very shy and could only whisper, "Don't know."

"'Course he knows!" said his sister. "He said it just before you came. Go on, tell the carpenter."

"A top," whispered the little boy.

"That's easy," said the carpenter, and in no time at all he had made a top.

"And now you must make something for Mother!" said the children. Mother Christmas had been watching, but all the time she held something behind her back.

"Shush, children, don't keep bothering the carpenter," she said.

"That's all right," said Anderson. "What would you like me to make?"

Mother Christmas brought out the thing she was holding; it was a wooden ladle, very worn, with a crack in it.

"Could you mend this for me, d'you think?" she asked.

"Hm, hm!" said Anderson, scratching his head with his carpenter's pencil. "I think I'd better make you a new one." And he quickly cut a new ladle for Mother Christmas. Then he found a long twisted root with a crook at one end and started stripping it with his knife. But although the children asked him and asked him he wouldn't tell them what it was going to be. When it was finished he held it up; it was a very distinguished-looking walking stick.

"Here you are, Grandpa!" he shouted to the old man, and handed him the stick. Then he gathered up all the chips and made a wonderful little bird with wings outspread to hang over the baby's cot.

"How pretty!" exclaimed Mother Christmas and all the children. "Thank the carpenter nicely now. We'll certainly never forget this Christmas Eve, will we?"

"Thank you, Mr Carpenter, thank you very much!" shouted the children.

Grandfather Christmas himself came stumping across the room leaning on his new stick. "It's grand!" he said. "It's just grand!"

There was the sound of feet stamping the snow off outside the door, and Anderson knew it was time for him to go. He said goodbye all round and wished them a Happy Christmas. Then he crawled through the narrow opening under the fallen tree. Father Christmas was waiting for him. He had the sledge and the empty sack with him.

"Thank you for your help, Anderson," he said. "What did the youngsters say when they saw you?"

"Oh, they seemed very pleased. Now they're just waiting for you to come home and see their new toys. How did you get on at my house? Was little Peter frightened of you?"

"Not a bit," said Father Christmas. "He thought I was you. 'Sit on Dadda's knee,' he kept saying."

"Well, I must go back to them," said Anderson, and said goodbye to Father Christmas.

When he got home, the first thing he said to the children was, "Can I see the presents you got from Father Christmas?"

But the children laughed. "Silly! You've seen them already — when you were Father Christmas; you unpacked them all for us!"

"What would you say if I told you I had been with Father Christmas's family all this time?"

But the children laughed again. "You wouldn't say anything so silly!"

they said, and they didn't believe him. So the carpenter came to me and asked me to write down the story, which I did.

WHY THE SEA IS SALT

NORWEGIAN FOLKTALE

Translated by George Webbe Dasent

Once on a time, but it was a long, long time ago, there were two brothers, one rich and one poor. Now, one Christmas Eve, the poor one hadn't so much as a crumb in the house, either of meat or bread, so he went to his brother to ask him for something to keep Christmas with, in God's name. It was not the first time his brother had been forced to help him, and you may fancy he wasn't very glad to see his face, but he said —

"If you will do what I ask you to do, I'll give you a whole flitch of bacon."

So the poor brother said he would do anything, and was full of thanks.

"Well, here is the flitch," said the rich brother, "and now go straight to Hell."

"What I have given my word to do, I must stick to," said the other; so he took the flitch and set off. He walked the whole day, and at dusk he came to a place where he saw a very bright light.

"Maybe this is the place," said the man to himself. So he turned aside, and the first thing he saw was an old, old man, with a long white beard, who stood in a shed, hewing wood for the Christmas fire.

"Good even," said the man with the flitch.

"The same to you; whither are you going so late?" said the man.

"Oh! I'm going to Hell, if I only knew the right way," answered the poor man.

"Well, you're not far wrong, for this is Hell," said the old man; "when you get inside they will be all for buying your flitch, for meat is scarce in Hell; but mind, you don't sell it unless you get the hand-quern which stands behind the door for it. When you come out, I'll teach you how to handle the quern, for it's good to grind almost anything."

So the man with the flitch thanked the other for his good advice, and gave a great knock at the Devil's door.

When he got in, everything went just as the old man had said. All the devils, great and small, came swarming up to him like ants round an anthill, and each tried to outbid the other for the flitch.

"Well!" said the man, "by rights my old dame and I ought to have this flitch for our Christmas dinner; but since you have all set your hearts on it, I suppose I must give it up to you; but if I sell it at all, I'll have for it that quern behind the door yonder."

At first the Devil wouldn't hear of such a bargain, and chaffered and haggled with the man; but he stuck to what he said, and at last the Devil had to part with his quern. When the man got out into the yard, he asked the old woodcutter how he was to handle the quern; and after he had learned how to use it, he thanked the old man and went off home as fast as he could, but still the clock had struck twelve on Christmas Eve before he reached his own door.

"Wherever in the world have you been?" said his old dame; "here have I sat hour after hour waiting and watching, without so much as two sticks to lay together under the Christmas brose*."

"Oh!" said the old man, "I couldn't get back before, for I had to go a long way first for one thing, and then for another; but now you shall see what you shall see."

So he put the quern on the table, and bade it first of all grind lights, then a tablecloth, then meat, then ale, and so on till they had got everything that was nice for Christmas fare. He had only to speak the word, and the quern

* porridge

66

ground out what he wanted. The old dame stood by blessing her stars, and
kept on asking where he had got this wonderful quern, but he wouldn't tell
her.

"It's all one where I got it from; you see the quern is a good one, and the
mill-stream never freezes, that's enough."

So he ground meat and drink and dainties enough to last out till Twelfth
Day, and on the third day he asked all his friends and kin to his house, and
gave a great feast. Now, when his rich brother saw all that was on the table,
and all that was behind in the larder, he grew quite spiteful and wild, for he
couldn't bear that his brother should have anything.

"'Twas only on Christmas Eve," he said to the rest, "he was in such
straits that he came and asked for a morsel of food in God's name, and now
he gives a feast as if he were count or king"; and he turned to his brother and
said —

"But whence, in Hell's name, have you got all this wealth?"

"From behind the door," answered the owner of the quern, for he didn't
care to let the cat out of the bag. But later on the evening, when he had got a
drop too much, he could keep his secret no longer, and brought out the quern
and said —

"There, you see what has gotten me all this wealth"; and so he made the
quern grind all kinds of things. When his brother saw it, he set his heart on
having the quern, and, after a deal of coaxing, he got it; but he had to pay
three hundred dollars for it, and his brother bargained to keep it till hay-
harvest, for he thought, "If I keep it till then, I can make it grind meat and
drink that will last for years." So you may fancy the quern didn't grow rusty
for want of work, and when hay-harvest came, the rich brother got it, but the
other took care not to teach him how to handle it.

It was evening when the rich brother got the quern home, and next morning he told his wife to go out into the hay field and toss, while the mowers
cut the grass, and he would stay at home and get the dinner ready. So, when

dinner-time drew near, he put the quern on the kitchen table and said, —

"Grind herrings and broth, and grind them good and fast."

So the quern began to grind herrings and broth; first of all, all the dishes full, then all the tubs full, and so on till the kitchen floor was quite covered. Then the man twisted and twirled at the quern to get it to stop, but for all his twisting and fingering the quern went on grinding, and in a little while the broth rose so high that the man was like to drown. So he threw open the kitchen door and ran into the parlour, but it wasn't long before the quern had ground the parlour full too, and it was only at the risk of his life that the man could get hold of the latch of the house door through the stream of broth. When he got the door open, he ran out and set off down the road, with the stream of herrings and broth at his heels, roaring like a waterfall over the whole farm.

Now, his old dame, who was in the field tossing hay, thought it a long time to dinner, and at last she said —

"Well! though the master doesn't call us home, we may as well go. Maybe he finds it hard work to boil the broth, and will be glad of my help."

The men were willing enough, so they sauntered homewards; but just as they had got a little way up the hill, what should they meet but herrings, and broth, and bread, all running and dashing, and splashing together in a stream, and the master himself running before them for his life, and as he passed them he bawled out, — "Would to heaven each of you had a hundred throats! but take care you're not drowned in the broth."

Away he went, as though the Evil One were at his heels, to his brother's house, and begged him for God's sake to take back the quern that instant; for, said he —

"If it grinds only one hour more, the whole parish will be swallowed up by herrings and broth."

But his brother wouldn't hear of taking it back till the other paid him down three hundred dollars more.

So the poor brother got both the money and the quern, and it wasn't long before he set up a farmhouse far finer than the one in which his brother lived, and with the quern he ground so much gold that he covered it with plates of gold; and as the farm lay by the seaside, the golden house gleamed and glistened far away over the sea. All who sailed by put ashore to see the rich man in the golden house, and to see the wonderful quern, the fame of which spread far and wide, till there was nobody who hadn't heard tell of it.

So one day there came a skipper who wanted to see the quern; and the first thing he asked was if it could grind salt.

"Grind salt!" said the owner; "I should just think it could. It can grind anything."

When the skipper heard that, he said he must have the quern, cost what it would; for if he only had it, he thought he should be rid of his long voyages across stormy seas for a lading of salt. Well, at first the man wouldn't hear of parting with the quern; but the skipper begged and prayed so hard, that at last he let him have it, but he had to pay many, many thousand dollars for it. Now, when the skipper had got the quern on his back, he soon made off with it, for he was afraid lest the man should change his mind; so he had no time to ask how to handle the quern, but got on board his ship as fast as he could, and set sail. When he had sailed a good way off, he brought the quern on deck and said —

"Grind salt, and grind both good and fast."

Well, the quern began to grind salt so that it poured out like water; and when the skipper had got the ship full, he wished to stop the quern, but whichever way he turned it, and however much he tried, it was no good; the quern kept grinding on, and the heap of salt grew higher and higher, and at last down sunk the ship.

There lies the quern at the bottom of the sea, and grinds away at this very day, and that's why the sea is salt.

THE POOR COUNT'S CHRISTMAS

FRANK STOCKTON

Very many years ago there lived a noble Count, who was one of the kindest and best-hearted men in the world. Every day in the year, he gave to the poor and helped the friendless, but it was at the merry Christmastime that his goodness shone brightest. He had even vowed a vow, that, as far as he was able to make them so, every child he knew should be happy on Christmas Day.

Early every Christmas morning, each boy and girl in the neighborhood, who was old enough, and not too old, came to the castle of the Count Cormo, and there the Count and the Countess welcomed them all, rich or poor, and through the whole day there were games, and festive merry-making, and good things to eat, and fun of every kind, and besides all this, there was a grand Christmas tree, with a present on it for each of the eager, happy youngsters who stood around it.

But although the good Count had a castle and rich lands, he gave away so much money that he became poorer and poorer, so that at last he and his wife often found it hard to get the clothes and food they absolutely needed.

But this made no difference with the Christmas festivities. The Count was not now able to be very generous during the year, although he was always willing to divide a meal with a hungry person; but he managed so that the children could have their festival and their presents at Christmas.

Year by year he had sold for this purpose some of the beautiful things which the castle contained, so that now there was scarcely enough furniture left for the actual use of himself and the Countess.

One night, about a week before Christmas, the Count and his wife sat in the great hall before a fire smaller and poorer than those which burned on the hearth of most of the cottagers in the surrounding country, for the cottagers could go into the woods and pick up sticks and twigs, whereas the Count had sold all his forests, so that he could not cut wood, and he had only one old man for outdoor work, and he had already picked up all the fallen branches within a wide circuit of the castle.

"Well, one thing is certain," said the Countess Cormo, as she drew her chair nearer to the little pile of burning sticks, "and that is, that we cannot have the children here at Christmas this year."

"Why not?" asked the Count.

"Because we have nothing to give them," replied his wife. "We have nothing for them to eat; nothing to put on the tree, and no money to buy anything. What would be the good of their coming when we have nothing at all for them?"

"But we must have something," said the Count. "Think of all the years that we have had these Christmas gatherings, and then think how hard it would be, both for us and the little ones, to give them up now we are growing old; and we may not be with the children another year. There are yet several days before Christmas; I can sell something tomorrow, and we can have the tree and everything prepared in time. There will not be so much to eat as usual, and the presents will be smaller, but it will be our good old Christmas in spite of that."

"I should like very much to know what you are going to sell," asked the Countess. "I thought we had already parted with everything that we could possibly spare."

"Not quite," said the Count. "There is our old family bedstead. It is very

72

large; it is made of the most valuable woods, and it is inlaid with gold and silver. It will surely bring a good price."

"Sell the family bedstead!" cried the Countess. "The bedstead on which your ancestors, for generations, have slept and died! How could you even think of such a thing! And what are we going to sleep on, I'd like to know?"

"Oh, we can get along very well," said the Count. "There is a small bedstead which you can have, and I will sleep upon the floor. I would much rather do that than have the children disappointed at Christmastime."

"On the floor! at your age!" exclaimed the Countess. "It will be the death of you! But if you have made up your mind, I suppose there is no use in my saying anything more about it."

"Not the least in the world," replied her husband, with a smile; and so she said no more.

It was on the morning of the next day that there came through the forest, not very far from the Count Cormo's castle, a tall young giant. As he strode along, he appeared to be talking to the forefinger of his right hand, which he held up before him. He was not, however, talking to his forefinger, but to a little fairy who was sitting on it, chatting away in a very lively manner.

"And so," said this little creature, "you are two hundred miles from your own home! What in the world made you take so long a journey?"

"I don't call it very long," replied the giant; "and I had to take it. There was nothing else to do. You see I have nothing to eat, or almost nothing, in my castle, and a person can't get along that way. He must go and see about things."

"And what are you going to see about?" asked the fairy.

"I am going to see if my grandfather's uncle is dead. He is very rich and I am one of his heirs. When I get my share of his money, I shall be quite comfortable."

"It seems to me," said the fairy, "that it is a very poor way of living, to be waiting for other people's money."

"It is so," replied the giant. "I'm tired of it. I've been waiting ever since I was a little boy."

The fairy saw that her companion had not exactly understood her remark, but she said no more about it. She merely added, "It seems strange to hear you say that you once were little."

"Oh, yes, I was," said the giant. "At one time, I was no taller than a horse."

"Astonishing!" said the fairy, making believe to be very much surprised. "Now, when I was a baby, I was about the size of a pea."

This made the giant laugh, but he said he supposed it must have been so, considering the present size, and then he said: "Talking of peas reminds me that I am hungry. We must stop somewhere, and ask for something to eat."

"That will suit me very well, but don't let us go to the same place," said the fairy. "I expect you are dreadfully hungry."

"All right," replied the other. "There is a great house over in the valley, not more than fifteen miles away. I'll just step over there, and you can go to Count Cormo's castle. I'll take you to the edge of the woods. When you've had your dinner, come back to this big oak, and I will meet you; I've heard the Count is getting very poor, but he'll have enough for you."

So the giant put the fairy down on the ground, and she skipped along to the castle, while he stepped over to the house in the valley.

In an hour or two they met again at the great oak, and the giant taking up his little friend on his forefinger, they continued their journey.

"You told me that Count Cormo was poor," she said, "but I don't believe you know how poor he really is. When I went there, he and his wife had just finished their dinner, and were sitting before the fireplace. I didn't notice any fire in it. They were busy talking, and so I did not disturb them, but just climbed up on the table to see what I could find to eat. You haven't any idea what a miserable meal they must have had. Of course there was enough left for me, for I need only a few crumbs, but everything was so hard and stale that I could scarcely eat it. I don't see how they can live in that way. But after

75

the meal, when I heard them talking, I found out how poor they really were."

"It wasn't exactly the proper thing to sit there and listen to them, was it?" asked the giant.

"Perhaps not," said the fairy, "but I did want to hear what they were saying. So I sat quite still. They were talking about the Christmas tree, and all the other good things they give the children every year; and although they are so poor, they are going to do just the same this year."

"I don't see how they can," said the giant.

"The Count is going to sell his family bedstead," replied his companion.

The young giant stopped short in the path.

"You don't mean to say," he exclaimed, "that the celebrated family bedstead of the Cormo family is to be sold to give the children a Christmas tree!"

"That is exactly what I mean," replied the fairy.

"Well, well, well!" said the giant, resuming his walk. "I never heard of such a thing in all my born days. It's dreadful, it's pitiful!"

"Indeed it is," said the fairy.

"It ought to be stopped," added the giant. "He shouldn't be allowed to do such a thing."

"Indeed he shouldn't," the fairy said.

And thus they went on lamenting and regretting the poor Count's purpose, for about eleven miles. Then they came to a crossroad through the forest.

"I'll go down here," said the giant, "and leave you among your friends at Fairy Elms, where you want to go."

"I'm not sure that I do want to go there just now," said the fairy. "I think I should like to go with you to your grandfather's uncle's castle, and see what your prospects are. If you find he is still alive, shall you wait?"

"I guess not," said the giant, laughing. "But you can come along with me, and we'll see how things stand."

Before very long, they came to a great castle, and a warder stood before the gate.

"Ho, warder!" cried the giant when he came up. "How goes it with my grandfather's uncle, the old giant Omscrag?"

"He has been dead a month," said the warder, "and his property is all divided among his heirs."

"That is not so," roared the giant. "I am one of his heirs, and I haven't got anything."

"I don't know anything about it," said the warder. "I was told to give that message to everyone who came, and I've given it to you."

"Who told you to give it?" cried the giant.

"My master, Katofan, who is the old giant's principal heir, and who now owns the castle."

"Katofan!" exclaimed the giant. "What impudence! He's a ninth cousin by marriage. Where is he? I want to see him."

"I don't think he is well enough to see anybody today," said the warder.

"Open that gate!" the giant roared, "or I shall plunge your family into woe!"

The warder turned pale, and opened the gate as wide as it would go, while the giant, with the fairy on his finger, walked boldly in.

In a large inner hall, sitting before a great fire, they saw a giant so tall and thin that he looked as if he had been made of great fishing-poles. He turned uneasily in his chair when he saw his visitor, and was going to say something about being too unwell to receive company, when our young giant, whose name was Feldar, interrupted him by calling out, in a tremendous voice:

"Well, now, Katofan, I should like to know what all this means! How did you come to be heir to this castle?"

"Because it descended to me from my good old relative and friend," said the other.

"I expect there are a hundred heirs, who have a better right to it than you," said our giant. "The truth is, no doubt, that you were here when my grandfather's uncle died, and that you took possession, and have since kept everybody out."

"Oh, no," said the thin giant, "the other heirs have had a share of the fortune."

"How many of them?" said Feldar, "and how much did they get?"

"As many as two or three of them," said the other, "and they got some very nice things in the way of ornaments and curiosities."

"Well," said Feldar, stretching himself up high, "I am one of the heirs to this property, and I want my share of it. Who attends to the dividing business? Do you do it yourself?"

"Oh, no!" said the thin giant. "I am not well enough for that. I cannot go about much. But I will send for my dividing-agent. I had to employ one, there was so much to do. He will see that you get your share."

He then rang a bell, and a small man appeared. When the fairy saw him, she could not help laughing, but her laugh was such a little one that no one noticed it. He had a bushy head of hair, which was black as ink on one side, and as white as milk on the other. Looking at him from one side, he seemed quite young, and from the other side, quite old.

"Flipkrak," said the thin giant, "this is another heir to this property; we overlooked him when we made our division. I wish you would take him, as you did the others, and let him choose something that he would like to have."

"Certainly," said Flipkrak. "This way, good sir," and he went out of a side-door, followed closely by Feldar.

"How would you like a hinge?" cried the thin giant, as they reached the door. "There are some very handsome and odd hinges, nearly new. If you take one, you might some day get another to match it, and then you would have a nice pair all ready, when you put up a new door."

Feldar stopped a moment in the doorway.

"I'll look at them," he answered, and then went on.

"Here, good sir," said Flipkrak, showing the young giant into a large room, "is a collection of most beautiful articles. You can choose any one of them, or even two if you like. They will be admirable mementos of your deceased relative."

Feldar looked around. There were all sorts of brass and iron ornaments, old pieces of furniture, and various odds and ends, of little value.

"A nice lot of rubbish," said the young giant. "If I ever have any holes to fill up, on my ground, I may send for a few wagon-loads of it. Suppose we look through the rest of the castle?"

"Oh, good sir," said the dividing-agent, "the things in the rest of the castle belong to my good master!"

"You can come, if you choose," said Feldar, striding away, "or you can stay behind," and the poor man, frightened, ran after him as fast as he could.

The young giant walked through several of the vast rooms of the castle. "I see you have a great deal of very fine furniture here," he said to Flipkrak, "and I need furniture. I will mark some of it with this piece of chalk, and you can send it to me."

"Oh, yes, good sir," cried the dividing-agent, quite pleased at this. "We can send it to you after you go away."

Feldar took a piece of chalk from his pocket, and marked enough furniture to furnish an ordinary castle.

"This kind of chalk will not rub off," he said, "and I've marked the things where it won't show. But don't overlook any of them. Now, where are your money-vaults?"

"Oh, good sir!" cried the dividing-agent, "you can't go there, we don't divide any of — I mean we haven't any money-vaults!"

"Give me the key," said Feldar.

"Oh, good sir!" cried Flipkrak, shaking with terror, "I must not let that go out of my keeping — I mean I haven't got it."

The giant made no answer, but taking the dividing-agent by the heels, he held him upside down in the air, and shook him. A big key dropped from his pockets.

"That's the key, no doubt," said the giant, putting the man down, and picking up the key. "I can find the vault by myself. I won't trouble you any more."

But as he went down to the lower parts of the castle, the dividing-agent ran after him, wailing and tearing his two-colored hair.

When he reached the money-vault, Feldar easily opened the door and walked in. Great bags of gold and silver, each holding about a bushel, were piled up around the walls. Feldar took out his piece of chalk and marked about a dozen of those bags which held the gold coin.

"Oh, that's right, good sir," cried Flipkrak, feeling a little better. "We can send them to you after you go away."

"What is in those small bags, on that shelf?" asked Feldar.

"Those are diamonds, good sir," said the agent; "you can mark some of them if you like."

"I will mark one," said the giant to the fairy, who was securely nestled in the ruffles of his shirt-bosom, "and that I will give to you."

"To me!" exclaimed Flipkrak, who did not see the fairy; "what does he mean by that?"

"Thank you," said the little creature in delight. "Diamonds are so lovely! How glad I am that your grandfather's uncle died!"

"You shouldn't say that," said the giant. "It isn't proper."

"But you feel glad, don't you?" she asked.

"I don't talk about it, if I do," said Feldar. Then turning to the dividing-agent, he told him that he thought he had marked all the bags he wanted.

"All right, good sir," said Flipkrak, "we will send them to you, very soon — very soon."

"Oh, you needn't trouble yourself about that," said Feldar; "I will take them along with me." And so saying, he put the bag of diamonds in one of his coat-pockets, and began to pile the bags of money on his shoulders.

The dividing-agent yelled and howled with dismay, but it was of no use. Feldar loaded himself with his bags, and walked off, without even looking at Flipkrak, who was almost crazy at seeing so much of his master's treasure boldly taken away from him.

Feldar stopped for a moment in the great hall, where the thin giant was still sitting before the fire. "I've taken my share of the money," he said, "and I've marked a lot of furniture and things which I want you to send me, inside of a week. Do you understand?"

The thin giant gave one look at the piles of bags on Feldar's shoulders, and fainted away. He had more money left than he could possibly use, but he could not bear to lose the least bit of the wealth he had seized upon.

"What in the world are you going to do with all that money?" the fairy asked.

"I am going to give one bag of it to Count Cormo, so that he can offer the children a decent Christmas tree, and the rest I shall carry to my castle on Shattered Crag."

"I don't believe the Count will take it," said the fairy. "He's awfully proud, and he would say that you were giving the Christmas feasts and not he. I wish you would let me manage this affair for you."

"Well, I will," said the giant.

"All right," cried the fairy, clapping her hands. "I'll do the thinking, and you can do the working. It's easy for me to think."

"And it's just as easy for me to work," said Feldar, with hearty goodwill.

The day before Christmas, poor Count Cormo sat, quite disconsolate, in his castle-hall, before a hearth where there was no fire. He had sold his family bedstead, but he had received very little money for it. People said such old bedsteads were not worth much, even if they were inlaid with precious metals. So he had been able only to prepare a small tree, on which he had hung the cheapest kind of presents, and his feast was very plain and simple. The Countess, indeed, was afraid the things would not go around, for their old servant had told them that he had heard there would be more children at the castle the next day than had ever been there before. She was in favor of giving up the whole affair and of sending the children home as soon as they should come.

"What is the use," she said, "of having them here, when we have so little to give them? They will get more at home; and then if they don't come we shall have the things for ourselves."

"No, no, my dear," said the Count; "this may be the last time that we shall have the children with us, for I do not see how we can live much longer in this sorrowful condition, but the dear girls and boys must come tomorrow. I should not wish to die knowing that we had missed a Christmas. We must do the best with what we have, and I am sure we can make them happy if we try. And now let us go to bed, so as to be up early tomorrow."

The Countess sighed. There was only one little bedstead, and the poor Count had to sleep on the floor.

Christmas Day dawned bright, clear and sparkling. The Count was in good spirits.

"It is a fine day," he said to his wife, "and that is a great thing for us."

"We need all we can get," said the Countess, "and it is well for us that fine days do not cost anything."

Very soon the Count heard the sound of many merry voices, and his eyes began to sparkle.

"They are coming!" he cried, and threw open the door of the castle, and went to meet his little guests; but when he saw them he started back.

"What do you think?" he exclaimed to the Countess, who stood behind him. "There is a long procession of them, and they are headed by a giant — the young giant Feldar! Who ever heard of such a thing as a giant coming to a children's festival! He will eat up everything we have in a few mouthfuls!"

"You might as well let him do it!" said the Countess. "There won't be enough for the others, anyway. There seem to be hundreds of them; and if there isn't a band of music striking up!"

Sure enough, quite a procession was approaching the castle. First came the giant Feldar, with Tillette, the little fairy, on his finger; then four or five musicians; and after them a long line of children, all dressed in their best clothes, and marching two by two.

"Merry Christmas!" shouted the giant, as soon as he saw the Count Cormo, and then all the children shouted "Merry Christmas!" until the castle courtyard echoed with the cheerful greeting, while the band played loudly and merrily.

"Come in, my dears," cried the Count to the children. "I am glad to see you. But as for you, good giant, I fear my door is not quite large enough. But perhaps you can stoop and squeeze yourself in."

"Count Cormo!" cried the fairy, from the giant's finger. "I have a plan to propose."

The good Count looked up in surprise.

"If it isn't a dear little fairy!" he exclaimed. "Why, certainly, if you have a plan to propose, I shall be happy to hear it."

"Well, then," said Tillette, "suppose we go first into the great hall in the old wing of the castle. That is so large that it will hold us all, and we can have a grand dance, if we feel like it, after we get there."

"I am afraid that the great hall would be very uncomfortable," said the Count. "No one has ever lived in it, nor even entered it, so far as I know, for many years; and everything must be covered with dust and cobwebs."

"But it would be so nice to march around that great hall with the music and everything. I don't believe there's any dust."

"Well, then," said the Count, "as you seem to have set your heart on it, we'll go."

So the Count and the Countess put on their hats and took their places in the procession, at the head of the line of children and just behind the musicians. Then they all marched across the great courtyard to the old wing of the castle, and when they reached the doors of the great hall, the giant swung them open, and everybody entered.

Never were there two such astonished people as the Count and Countess!

Right in the middle of the hall stood a great Christmas tree, which the giant had brought in on his shoulders from the woods. On the wide-spreading branches of this tall tree were hung hundreds of presents and sparkling ornaments.

"What does this mean?" gasped the Count. "Whose tree is this?"

"It is yours! It is yours!" cried all the children in a merry chorus which made the old walls ring. "It is your Christmas tree, and we, the children, who love you, give it to you!"

The Count looked around from one to another of the children, but did not say a word. His heart was too full for him to speak. Then the giant put the fairy on his shirt-frill, and, stooping down, took up the Count and Countess, one in each hand, holding them gently, but very firmly, and carried them around the tree, raising them up and down, so that they could see all the presents, even those at the very top.

Everything was labeled — not with the name of the person they were for, for they were all for the Count and Countess, but with the names of those who gave them.

Presently, the Count began to read out every name aloud, and each time a child's name was called, all the other children would clap and cheer. There were a good many small bags, which looked as if they were very heavy, hanging here and there, and these were all marked "From Feldar", while some beautiful clusters of diamonds, which glittered in the sunlight that poured in through the windows, were labeled "From Tillette."

It took a long time to look at all the presents, which were rather different

84

from the things generally seen on Christmas trees, for the great branches and boughs held every kind of useful and ornamental articles that the Count and Countess needed. Many of these were old family treasures which they once had owned, but had been obliged to sell, to keep up their Christmas festivals.

The Count and his wife were more and more delighted as they were carried around the tree, but at last this happy business was over, and the giant put them down upon the floor.

"Now for a dance!" cried the fairy, in her clear little voice, and the music struck up, while all the children began to dance gaily around the tree.

The Count and Countess, with the giant and fairy, stood aside, while this happy play was going on, enjoying it almost as much as the children, but when the dancing began to flag, the Count thought that the time had now come when the party ought to have something to eat, and his heart failed him when he thought of the very meager repast he had to offer them.

But he need not have troubled his mind about that. As soon as the dance was done, the giant stepped to a door which led to another apartment, and throwing it open he cried:

"Enter the banqueting hall! This is the feast the children give to the good Count Cormo and his wife. He has feasted them often and often, and made them happy, for many a Christmas. It is their turn now."

Everybody trooped through the door, the children gently pushing the Count and Countess before them. The room was truly a banqueting hall. A long table was covered with every kind of thing good to eat, and, on smaller tables in the corners, was ever so much more, in case it should be needed. Here and there, on the long table, were enormous cakes, great bowls of jelly, and vast pies. Everybody knew these were for the giant.

The Count and Countess took their places at the head and foot of the table; and all the children gathered around, and everybody had a splendid appetite. Just in the center of the table there was a little table about three inches high, on which there were dear little morsels of the dainties the others were eating. At this table, on a little chair, the fairy Tillette sat, where she could see everything, and she enjoyed herself as much as anybody else did.

When the banquet was over, they all went into the great hall, where they had dances and games and singing, and there never was a merrier company before.

When evening approached, the Count stood up and made a little speech. He tried to tell the children how good he thought they were, and how happy they had made him. He did not say much, but they all understood him. When he had finished, there was a silence over the whole room. The children looked at one another, some of them smiled, and then, all together, as if they had planned it out before, they cried:

"The giant and the fairy did it all. He gave us the money and she told us what to buy."

"Oh, pshaw!" said the young giant, his face turning very red; "I thought nothing was to be said about that," and he went outside so that nobody should make a speech to him.

Now all the children came up, and each in turn bade the Count and Countess farewell, and then, headed by the giant's band of music, and singing merrily, they marched away to their homes.

But Count Cormo would not let the giant and the fairy go away so soon. He made them come with him to the dwelling part of his castle, and there, after a little squeezing and stooping by the giant at the door, they all sat down around the hearth, on which a fine blazing fire had been built.

"I don't know what to say, my dear Feldar," said the Count, "and I can never repay you ——."

The giant was just about to exclaim that the Count need not say anything, and that he did not wish to be repaid, when, seeing he felt embarrassed, the fairy broke in:

"Oh, yes, dear Count, you can repay him. You can adopt him. You have no

children, you are getting old, and are living alone. He has no parents —
even his grandfather's uncle is now dead — and he lives all by himself in
his castle on the Shattered Crag. He is rich, and you can show him how to
do good with his great wealth. He could come and live in the old wing of the
castle, where the rooms are so large; the furniture he has inherited could be
sent here, and you could all be so happy together! Will you take him?"

The Count's eyes filled with tears.

"Would you like us to adopt you?" he said to Feldar.

"Indeed I should," was the reply. Then the young giant kneeled on the
floor; and the Count got up on a table, and put his hands on the young
giant's head, and adopted him.

"Now you ought to adopt her," said Feldar, after he had kissed the Count
and Countess, and had sat down again by the fire.

"No," said Tillette, "I cannot be adopted. But I will often come to see you,
and we shall be happy together, and the children will have a splendid
Christmas festival every year."

"As long as we live," said the Count and Countess.

"As long as I live," said Feldar.

When the Count and Countess went up to their room, that night, there
they found the family bedstead, all cleaned and polished, with its gold and
silver ornaments sparkling like new.

"What a happy Christmas I have had!" said good Count Cormo.

BABUSHKA AND THE THREE WISE MEN

RUSSIAN LEGEND

Retold by Norah Montgomerie

Once upon a time, three Wise Men were travelling across the country with gifts for the great King who was soon to be born. Tired and hungry, they stopped at a little cottage and asked for food and shelter. The good Babushka opened her door wide and told them to make themselves comfortable by the fire while she prepared a meal for them. The three Wise Men thanked her and accepted her hospitality.

As they ate the meal she had made for them, they told her that they were following a star which would lead them to the place where the King of Kings was to be born, and that they were carrying gifts for Him. Babushka listened to them.

"How I would like to greet the Little One too," she said.

"Come with us then," said the three Wise Men. "We shall leave as soon as the stars are bright in the sky."

"I can't leave my cottage until I have cleaned and swept it, and then of course I will have to prepare for the journey. But I will come as soon as I'm ready."

When the stars were bright in the sky, the three Wise Men said it was time for them to go but, as Babushka was not ready, they had to leave without her.

After they had gone Babushka cleared away the meal, washed up, and bustled about the house until everything was as neat and tidy as she could make it. Then she searched for gifts to take to the Little One, for she was sure she could not go empty-handed.

After that she scrubbed her face until it shone and took out her best Sunday clothes, and dressed herself very carefully, for was she not going to visit the King of Kings?

When she was quite sure everything was in good order, she locked the door of her cottage and set out along the road the Wise Men had taken.

But the star that had guided them had moved across the sky and was nowhere to be seen, and soon poor Babushka was lost. She tried this road and she tried that.

"I wish I had gone when I had the chance," she sighed. "I could have tidied the house some other time."

But it was too late, there was no sign to tell her which way to go, and although she wandered on and on she never found the stable where the King was born.

On Christmas morning, in Russia, when the children find toys and sweets in their stockings, they say, "See, what Babushka has left me!"

For they believe she is still wandering about on Christmas Eve, searching for the Little One in every house where there are children, and that she leaves gifts in all their stockings just to be sure she does not miss Him.

THE FIR TREE

HANS CHRISTIAN ANDERSEN

English version by Neil Philip

Out in the forest there was a pretty little fir tree. It had room to grow, and fresh air, and all the sun it could want, and plenty of bigger companions, both firs and pines. But the little fir tree was in such a tearing hurry to grow that it took no notice of the warm sunshine or the fresh air, and didn't give a second glance to the village children out gathering wild strawberries or raspberries. Sometimes when they had gathered the fruit they would sit down by the tree, and say, "What a sweet little tree!" But the tree had no time to listen to idle chatter.

By the next year the tree had grown taller, and the year after that it was bigger still — you could tell how old it was by counting the rings on its stem.

"Oh, if only I was as tall as the others," sighed the little fir tree. "Then I could spread my branches out, and look out from my top over the wide world. The birds would nest in my branches, and when the wind blew I could bow my head just as grandly as the others."

It took no pleasure in the sunshine, or the birds, or the rosy-tinted clouds that drifted overhead, morning and evening.

When winter came, and the sparkling snow lay all around, a hare might come bounding along and jump right over the little tree — it was *so* vexing! Two winters passed, and by the third, the tree was too tall, and the hares had

to run round it. Oh, to grow, to grow, and become tall and old — that was the only joy in life, thought the tree.

In the autumn the woodcutters used to come and fell some of the largest trees. It happened every year, and the young fir tree, now it was growing up, used to shudder when the mighty trees came crashing to the ground. With their branches lopped off you could hardly recognize them, they looked so thin and bare. They were loaded onto waggons and hauled away by horses.

Where were they going? What was going to happen to them?

In the spring, when the swallows and the stork arrived, the tree asked them, "Do you know where they've been taken? Have you seen them?"

The swallows didn't know anything, but the stork nodded wisely, and said, "I think I know. As I flew here from Egypt, I saw a lot of new ships, with splendid tall masts, and I daresay that was them — they certainly smelled of pine. You'd have been proud of them, they were standing so straight."

"Oh, I wish I were old enough to sail over the sea!" said the little tree. "By the way, what is the sea?"

"It's too big to explain," said the stork, and walked away.

"Enjoy your youth," said the sunbeams. "Have fun while you're growing up, and the fresh sap is rising in you. Rejoice in life!" And the wind caressed the tree, and kissed it, and the dew wept tears over it, but the little fir tree didn't understand why.

As Christmas drew near, some younger trees were cut down — some of them no bigger than the restless little fir tree, who so longed to be up and doing. These young trees — always the very handsomest ones — kept their branches. They too were loaded onto waggons and hauled away by horses.

"Where have they gone?" asked the fir tree. "They were no bigger than I am — in fact one was much smaller. Why did they keep their branches? Where will they end up?"

"We know! We know!" twittered the sparrows. "We peeped in at the windows in the town. We know where they are. Oh, you can't imagine the glory and fame! They've been planted in the middle of a warm room, and garlanded with beauty — golden apples, honey-cakes, toys, and hundreds of candles! We saw it."

"And then?" asked the fir tree, trembling in every branch. "And then? What happens then?"

"That's all we saw. But it was wonderful."

"I wonder if I will take that golden road," said the excited tree. "That would be even better than sailing on the sea. Oh, I wish Christmas would come again soon. I'm just as tall and branchy as the ones that were chosen. I wish I were on the waggon now, or standing in a warm room in all my glory. And then — then there must be something even more beautiful to come. Why else would they decorate me? Something even bigger and better will happen — but what will it be? Oh, I can't bear the waiting! I'm all of a fluster."

"Enjoy yourself with us," said the air and the sunshine. "Enjoy your youth and freedom."

But the fir tree couldn't be happy. It just kept on growing. It stayed dark green through the winter and summer, and people passing by would say, "What a handsome tree!"

That Christmas it was the first to be felled. The axe cut deep into its pith, and the tree fell to the earth with a sigh. It felt faint with pain, and quite forgot to be happy. It just felt sad at leaving its home, where its roots were. Never again would it see its friends, the bushes and flowers — perhaps not even the birds. There was no joy in such a parting.

The tree didn't come to itself until it was unloaded in a yard with the other trees, and heard a man say, "What a beauty — that's the one for us!"

Then two servants in full livery came and carried the tree into a grand room. There were portraits hanging on the walls, and by the big tile stove stood two enormous Chinese vases with lions on their lids. There were rocking-chairs, silk-covered sofas, and big tables covered with picture books and toys worth ever so much money — or so the children said. The tree was planted in a barrel filled with sand — but you couldn't see that it was a barrel because it was draped with green baize, and standing on a patterned rug. How the tree trembled! What was going to happen?

Then the servants and the young ladies of the family came to decorate it. On the branches they hung little nets cut out of fancy paper and filled with sweets; golden apples, and walnuts that hung down as if they grew there; and over a hundred red, blue, and white candles were fastened to the branches. Perched here and there were little dolls that looked just like people. And right at the top was a golden star made out of tinsel. It was glorious — quite glorious!

"Just wait for tonight," they all said. "Tonight it will really sparkle."

"If only it were tonight now," thought the tree. "If only the candles were lit. What will happen then? Will the trees come from the wood to admire me? Will the sparrows peep through the windows? Will I take root here, and keep my decorations winter and summer?"

That's what the fir tree thought. It gave itself a barkache from sheer longing — and a barkache for a tree is as nasty as a headache is for us.

At last the candles were lit. How they blazed! It made the tree tremble, so that one of the candles set fire to a branch. Oh, that hurt!

"Heavens!" cried the ladies, and put out the fire.

Now the tree didn't dare tremble — what a strain that was! But it was afraid of losing its decorations. It was quite dazed by all the brilliance.

Then the big doors opened, and the children came rushing in, as if they meant to knock the tree over. The adults followed more quietly, with the littlest ones, who stood quite silent for a moment, before shouting in delight and running round the tree. One by one the presents were taken down.

"What are they doing?" thought the tree. "What's going to happen now?"

When the candles had burned down, they were snuffed out, and then the children were allowed to plunder the tree. They rushed in so eagerly they made the branches creak — and if the tree hadn't been fixed to the ceiling at the top, where the gold star was, it would have toppled over.

The children danced round with their precious toys, and nobody took any notice of the tree, except their old nurse, who searched among the branches in case she could find an apple or a fig that the others had missed.

"A story! Let's have a story!" shouted the children, and they dragged a little fat man over to the tree. He sat down beneath it, saying, "Now we're in the wood   and besides, the tree might like to hear the story too. Now I'm only going to tell one, so which shall it be — Ivedy-Avedy, or Klumpy-Dumpy, who fell downstairs yet still came to the throne and married the princess?

Some of them shouted, "Ivedy-Avedy!" and some, "Klumpy-Dumpy!" There was a lot of screaming and shouting. Only the fir tree was silent, and it was thinking, "Is there something I should be doing?" But it had already done everything it was meant to do.

The little fat man told the story of Klumpy-Dumpy, who fell downstairs yet still came to the throne and married the princess. The children clapped their hands, and shouted, "Tell us another!" They wanted Ivedy-Avedy, too, but they only got Klumpy-Dumpy.

The fir tree just stood still, deep in its own thoughts. The birds in the forest had never told a story like that of Klumpy-Dumpy, who fell downstairs, yet still came to the throne and married the princess. "That's the kind of thing that happens in the world," thought the fir tree, who believed every word, because the storyteller was such a nice man. "Ah, who knows? Perhaps I'll fall downstairs too, and marry a princess!" And it looked forward to being decorated again next day with candles, toys, tinsel, and fruit.

"I shan't tremble tomorrow," it thought. "I'll enjoy it all. And I'll hear the story of Klumpy-Dumpy again, and maybe the one about Ivedy-Avedy, too." The tree spent all night wrapped in such thoughts.

Next morning the maids and servants came in.

"Now everything will begin again," thought the tree. But instead, they dragged it out of the room, up the stairs, and into the attic, where they stowed it away in a dark corner where the sun never shone.

"What's the meaning of this?" the tree asked itself. "What will I do here? What will I listen to?" And it leaned up against the wall, and stood there, thinking and thinking. It had plenty of time, as the days and nights passed by. No one came up there, and when at last someone did, it was only to put some old boxes up there. The tree was out of sight, and out of mind — utterly forgotten.

"It's winter now outside," thought the tree. "The ground will be hard, and covered with snow. Of course they can't plant me now, so I shall have to shelter here until spring. How thoughtful people are! If only it weren't so dark and lonely up here. There's not even a little hare. Those were good times, out in the forest, with the snow on the ground, and the hare bounding along — yes, even when he jumped right over me, though I didn't like it at the time. Up here it's so lonely."

"Squeak! Squeak!" said a little mouse, creeping along the floor, with another one behind it. The two mice sniffed at the fir tree, and clambered in and out among its branches. "It is dreadfully cold," they said. "But otherwise this is a fine place to be. Don't you think so, old tree?"

"Less of the 'old,'" said the fir tree. "There are lots of trees older than I am."

"Where do you come from?" asked the mice. "What do you know?" They were full of questions. "What's the most beautiful place on earth? Have you been there? Have you ever been to the larder, where the shelves are stacked with cheeses, and the ceiling is hung with hams — where you can dance on the tallow candles, and go in thin and come out fat?"

"Never heard of it," said the tree. "But I know the wood, where the sun shines, and the birds sing." And the tree told them all about its young days.

The mice had never heard anything like it. They listened closely, and said, "What a lot you've seen! How happy you must have been!"

"Me?" said the fir tree, and thought about what it had been saying. "Yes, I suppose they were good times." But then it told them about Christmas Eve, when it had been hung with sweets and candles.

"Ooh!" said the mice. "You have been a lucky old tree!"

"Less of the 'old,'" said the fir tree. "I've only this winter left the wood. I'm in my prime; it's only that I'm not growing just at the moment."

"What lovely stories you tell," said the little mice, and they came back the next night with four more mice who wanted to hear the fir tree tell stories. The more it told them, the more clearly it remembered everything, and thought, "Those really were good times — and they'll come again, they'll come again. Klumpy-Dumpy fell downstairs, yet still came to the throne and married the princess — perhaps I'll marry a princess, too." And then the fir tree thought of a pretty little birch tree growing out in the forest, that seemed like a princess to it.

"Who's Klumpy-Dumpy?" asked the little mice. So the fir tree told them the whole story. It could remember every single word. The little mice could have jumped to the top of the tree they were so happy. The next night, many more mice came, and on Sunday, even a couple of rats — but they said the story wasn't up to much, which made the mice sad, for now they didn't like it so well, either.

"Is that the only story you know?" asked the rats.

"The only one," replied the tree. "I heard it on the happiest night of my life, though at the time I didn't realize how happy I was."

"It's very boring! Don't you know any about bacon, or tallow candles? One about the larder?"

"No," said the tree.

"Then thanks for nothing," said the rats, and they went back home.

After that, the little mice stayed away too, and the tree sighed, "It really was nice when they all sat round me, those perky little mice, and listened to what I had to say. Now that's over too. I must remember to enjoy myself, when I'm taken out of here."

But when would that happen? It was one morning, when people came up and rummaged in the attic. The boxes were pulled aside, and the tree was dragged out. It's true they were rough with it, and one of the men pulled it straight away to the stairs and the daylight.

"My life's beginning again!" thought the tree. It could feel the fresh air, the sunshine — now it was out in the yard. Everything happened so quickly that the tree forgot to look at itself, there was so much else to see. The yard opened on to a garden where everything was in bloom. The sweet-smelling roses were rambling over a trellis, the lindens were in blossom, and the swallows were flying about, crying, "Kvirre-virre-vit — my husband's home!" But they didn't mean the fir tree.

"This is the life!" The tree shouted for joy, and stretched out its branches. But all its needles were withered and yellow. The tree had been thrown into a corner among the nettles. But the gold tinsel star was still fixed to its top, and it glittered in the bright sunshine.

Playing in the yard were some of the happy children who had danced around the tree at Christmas, and had so much fun. One of the youngest ran up and tore off the golden star.

"Look what I've found on that horrid old Christmas tree!" he shouted, stamping on its branches so that they snapped under his boots.

And the tree looked at the fresh garden and the beautiful flowers, and then at itself, and wished that it had stayed up in the dark attic. It thought of its young days in the wood, of that joyous Christmas Eve, and of the little mice who had listened so happily to the story of Klumpy-Dumpy.

"It's all over, all over!" said the poor tree. "I should have enjoyed myself while I had the chance. It's all over, over and done with!"

And a servant came and chopped the tree into small pieces, until there

was quite a pile. It made a fine blaze in the kitchen, and it groaned so loudly that every groan sounded like a pistol shot. That brought the children in from the yard: they sat round the fire, shouting "Bang! Bang!"

As it sighed and groaned, the tree thought of a summer's day in the forest, and a winter's night when the stars are shining. It thought of Christmas Eve, and Klumpy-Dumpy, the only story it had ever heard or knew how to tell — and so the tree was burned to ash.

The children went back to the yard to play, and the littlest had on his chest the gold star that the tree had worn on the happiest night of its life. That was all over now, and it was all over with the tree, and the story too. All stories must come to an end.

SCHNITZLE, SCHNOTZLE, AND SCHNOOTZLE

RUTH SAWYER

The Tirol straddles the Alps and reaches one hand into Italy and another into Austria. There are more mountains in the Tirol than you can count and every Alp has its story.

Long ago, some say on the Brenner-Alp, some say on the Mitterwald-Alp, there lived the king of all the goblins of the Tirol, and his name was Laurin. King Laurin. His kingdom was under the earth, and all the gold and silver of the mountains he owned. He had a daughter, very young and very lovely, not at all like her father, who had a bulbous nose, big ears, and a squat figure, and looked as old as the mountains. She loved flowers and was sad that none grew inside her father's kingdom.

"I want a garden of roses — red roses, pink roses, blush roses, flame roses, shell roses, roses like the sunrise and the sunset." This she said one day to her father. And the king laughed and said she should have just such a garden. They would roof it with crystal, so that the sun would pour into the depths of the kingdom and make the roses grow lovely and fragrant. The garden was planted and every rare and exquisite rose bloomed in it. And so much color they spread upwards on the mountains around that the snow caught it and the mortals living in the valley pointed at it with wonder. "What is it makes our Alps so rosy, so glowing?" they asked. And they spoke of it ever after as the alpen-glow.

103

I have told you this that you might know what kind of goblin King Laurin was. He was merry, and he liked to play pranks and have fun. He liked to go abroad into the valleys where the mortals lived, or pop into a herdsman's hut halfway up the mountain. There were men who said they had seen him — that small squat figure with a bulbous nose and big ears — gambolling with the goats on a summer day. And now I begin my story. It is an old one that Tirolese mothers like to tell their children.

Long ago there lived in one of the valleys a very poor cobbler indeed. His wife had died and left him with three children, little boys, all of them — Fritzl, Franzl and Hansl. They lived in a hut so small there was only one room in it, and in that was the cobbler's bench, a hearth for cooking, a big bed full of straw, and on the wall racks for a few dishes, and, of course, there was a table with a settle and some stools. They needed few dishes or pans, for there was never much to cook or eat. Sometimes the cobbler would mend the Sunday shoes of a farmer, and then there was good goats' milk to drink. Sometimes he would mend the holiday shoes of the baker, and then there was the good long crusty loaf of bread to eat. And sometimes he mended the shoes of the butcher, and then there was the good stew, cooked with meat in the pot, and noodles, leeks, and herbs. When the cobbler gathered the little boys around the table and they had said their grace, he would laugh and clap his hands and sometimes even dance. "Ha-ha!" he would shout. "Today we have the good . . . what? Ah-h . . . today we eat . . . Schnitzle, Schnotzle, and Schnootzle!"

With that he would swing the kettle off the hook and fill every bowl brimming full, and Fritzl, Franzl, and Hansl would eat until they had had enough. Ach, those were the good days — the days of having Schnitzle, Schnotzle, and Schnootzle. Of course, the cobbler was making up nonsense and nothing else, but the stew tasted so much better because of the nonsense.

Now a year came, with every month following his brother on leaden feet. The little boys and the cobbler heard the month of March tramp out and April tramp in. They heard June tramp out and July tramp in. And every month marched heavier than his brother. And that was because war was among them again. War, with workers taking up their guns and leaving mothers and children to care for themselves as best they could; and there was scant to pay even a poor cobbler for mending shoes. The whole village shuffled to church with the soles flapping and the heels lopsided, and the eyelets and buttons and straps quite gone.

Summer — that was not so bad. But winter came and covered up the good earth, and gone were the roots, the berries, the sorrel, and the corn. The tramp of November going out and December coming in was very loud indeed. The little boys were quite sure that the two months shook the hut as they passed each other on the mountainside.

As Christmas grew near, the little boys began to wonder if there would be any feast for them, if there would be the good father dancing about the room and laughing "Ha-ha," and singing "Ho-ho," and saying: "Now, this being Christmas Day we have the good . . . what?" And this time the little boys knew that they would never wait for their father to say it; they would shout themselves: "We know — it is the good Schnitzle, Schnotzle, and Schnootzle!" Ach, how very long it was since their father had mended shoes for the butcher! Surely — surely — there would be need soon again, with Christmas so near.

At last came the Eve of Christmas. The little boys climbed along the beginnings of the Brenner-Alp, looking for faggots. The trees had shed so little that year; every branch was green and grew fast to its tree, so few twigs had snapped, so little was there of dead, dried brush to fill their arms.

Their father came in when they had a small fire started, blowing his whiskers free of icicles, slapping his arms about his big body, trying to put warmth back into it. "Na-na, nobody will have a shoe mended today. I have asked everyone. Still there is good news. The soldiers are marching into the village. The inn is full. They will have boots that need mending, those soldiers. You will see." He pinched a cheek of each little boy; he winked at them and nodded his head. "You shall see — tonight I will come home with . . . what?"

"Schnitzle, Schnotzle, and Schnootzle," they shouted together, those three.

So happy they were they forgot there was nothing to eat for supper — not a crust, not a slice of cold porridge-pudding, not the smallest sup of goats' milk. "Will the soldiers have money to pay you?" asked Fritzl, the oldest.

"Not the soldiers, perhaps, but the captains. There might even be a general. I will mend the boots of the soldiers for nothing, for after all what day is coming tomorrow! They fight for us, those soldiers; we mend for them, ja? But a general — he will have plenty of money."

The boys stood about while their father put all his tools, all his pieces of leather into a rucksack; while he wound and wound and wound the woollen scarf about his neck, while he pulled the cap far down on his head. "It will be a night to freeze the ears off you," he said. "Now bolt the door after me, keep the fire burning with a little at a time; and climb into the straw-bed and pull the quilt over you. And let no one in!"

He was gone. They bolted the door; they put a little on the fire, they climbed into the big bed, putting Hansl, the smallest, in the middle. They pulled up the quilt, such a thin quilt to keep out so much cold! Straight and still and close together they lay, looking up at the little spot of light the fire made on the ceiling, watching their breath go upwards in icy spurts. With the going of the sun the wind rose. First it whispered: it whispered of good fires in big chimneys; it whispered of the pines on the mountainsides; it whispered of snow loosening and sliding over the glaciers. Then it began to blow: it blew hard, it blew quarrelsome, it blew cold and colder. And at last it roared. It roared its wintry breath through the cracks in the walls and under the door.

And Fritzl, Franzl and Hansl drew closer together and shivered.

"Whee . . . ooh . . . bang, bang! Whee . . . ooh . . . bang, bang!"

"Is it the wind or someone knocking?" asked Franzl.

"It is the wind," said Fritzl.

"Whee . . . ooh . . . knock, knock!"

"Is it the wind or someone knocking?" asked Hansl.

"It is the wind *and* someone knocking!" said Fritzl.

He rolled out of the bed and went to the window. It looked out directly on the path to the door. "Remember what our father said: do not open it," said Franzl.

But Fritzl looked and looked. Close to the hut, beaten against it by the wind, stood a little man no bigger than Hansl. He was pounding on the door. Now they could hear him calling: "Let me in! I tell you, let me in!"

"Oh, don't, don't!" cried Hansl.

"I must," said Fritzl. "He looks very cold. The wind is tearing at him as a wolf tears at a young lamb"; and with that he drew the bolt and into the hut skipped the oddest little man they had ever seen. He had a great peaked cap tied onto his head with deer thongs. He had a round red face out of which stuck a bulbous nose, like a fat plum on a pudding. He had big ears. And his teeth were chattering so hard they made the stools to dance. He shook his fist at the three little boys. "Ach, kept me waiting. Wanted to keep all the good food, all the good fire to yourselves? Na-na, that is no kind of hospitality."

He looked over at the little bit of a fire on the hearth, making hardly any heat in the hut. He looked at the empty table, not a bowl set or a spoon beside it. He took up the big pot, peered into it, turned it upside down to make sure nothing was clinging to the bottom, set it down with a bang. "So — you have already eaten it all. Greedy boys. But if you have saved no feast for me, you can at least warm me." With that he climbed into the big straw-bed with Franzl and Hansl, with his cap still tied under his chin. Fritzl tried to explain that they had not been greedy, that there had never been any food, not for days, to speak of. But he was too frightened of the little man, of his eyes as sharp and blue as ice, of his mouth so grumbling.

"Roll over, roll over," the little man was shouting at the two in the bed. "Can't you see I have no room? Roll over and give me my half of the quilt."

Fritzl saw that he was pushing his brothers out of the bed. "Na-na," he said, trying to make peace with their guest. "They are little, those two. There is room for all if we but lie quiet." And he started to climb into the bed himself, pulling gently at the quilt that there might be a corner for him.

But the little man bounced and rolled about shouting: "Give me room, give me more quilt. Can't you see I'm cold? I call this poor hospitality to bring a stranger inside your door, give him nothing to eat, and then grudge him bed and covering to keep him warm." He dug his elbow into the side of skinny little Hansl.

"Ouch!" cried the boy.

Fritzl began to feel angry. "Sir," he said "sir, I pray you to be gentle with my little brother. And I am sorry there has been nothing to give you. But our father, the cobbler, has gone to mend shoes for the soldiers. When he returns we look for food. Truly, this is a night to feast and to share. So if you will but lie still until he comes I can promise you . . ."

The little man rolled over and stuck his elbow into Fritzl's ribs. "Promise — promise. Na-na, what good is a promise? Come get out of bed and give me your place." He drew up his knees, put his feet in the middle of Fritzl's back and pushed with a great strength. The next moment the boy was spinning across the room. "There you go," roared the little man after him. "If you must keep warm turn cartwheels, turn them fast."

For a moment Fritzl stood sullenly by the small speck of fire. He felt bruised and very angry. He looked over at the bed. Sure enough, the greedy little man had rolled himself up in the quilt leaving only a short corner of it for the two younger boys. He had taken more than half of the straw for himself, and was even then pushing and digging at Hansl. He saw Franzl raise

himself up and take the place of his littlest brother, that he should get the digs.

Brrr . . . it was cold! Before he knew it Fritzl was doing as he had been told, turning cartwheels around the room. He had rounded the table and was coming toward the bed when — plop! Plop — plop — plop! Things were falling out of his pockets every time his feet swung high over his head. Plop — plop — plop! The two younger boys were sitting up in bed. It was their cries of astonishment which brought Fritzl's feet back to the floor again, to stay. In a circle about the room, he had left behind him a golden trail of oranges. Such oranges — big as two fists! And sprinkled everywhere between were comfits wrapped in gold and silver paper. Fritzl stood and gaped at them.

"Here, you, get out and keep warm yourself!" shouted the little man as he dug Franzl in the ribs. "Cartwheels for you, boy!" And the next minute Franzl was whirling in cartwheels about the room. Plop — plop — plop — things were dropping out of his pockets: Christmas buns, Christmas cakes covered with icing, with plums, with anise and caraway seeds.

The little man was digging Hansl now in the ribs. "Lazy boy, greedy boy. Think you can have the bed to yourself now? Na-na, I'll have it! Out you go!" And he put his feet against the littlest boy's back and pushed him onto the floor. "Cartwheels . . ." he began; but Fritzl, forgetting his amazement at what was happening, shouted: "But, sir, he is too little. He cannot turn . . ."

"Hold him up in the corner, then. You keep warmer when your heels are higher than your head. Step lively there. Take a leg, each of you, and be quick about it."

So angry did the little man seem, so fiery and determined, that Fritzl and Franzl hurried their little brother over to the chimney corner, stood him on his head and each held a leg. Donner and Blitzen! What happened then! Whack — whack — whickety-whack! Whack — whack — whickety-whack! Pelting the floor like hail against the roof came silver and gold pieces, all pouring out of Hansl's pockets.

Fritzl began to shout, Franzl began to dance. Hansl began to shout, "Let me down, let me down!" When they did the three little boys danced around the pile, taking hands, singing "Tra-la-la" and "Fiddle-de-dee" and "Ting-a-ling-a-ling," until their breath was gone and they could dance no longer. They looked over at the bed and Fritzl was opening his mouth to say: "Now, if you please, sir, we can offer you some Christmas cheer . . ." But the bed was empty, the quilt lay in a heap on the floor. The little man had gone.

The three little boys were gathering up the things on the floor — putting oranges into the big wooden bowl, buns and cakes on to the two platters, silver and gold pieces into this dish and that. And right in the midst of it in came their father, stamping, puffing in through the door. He had brought bread, he had brought milk, he had brought meat for the good stew — and noodles.

Such a wonder, such a clapping of hands, such a singing as they worked to get ready the Christmas feast! Fritzl began the story about their Christmas guest; Franzl told it mid-through; but little Hansl finished, making his brothers stand him in the corner again on his head to show just how it was that all the silver and gold had tumbled out of his pockets.

"Na-na," said the cobbler, "we are the lucky ones. I did not know it was true; always I thought it was a tale the grandfathers told the children. The saying goes that King Laurin comes every year at the Christmas to one hut — one family — to play his tricks and share his treasure horde."

"He was a very ugly little man," said Hansl. "He dug us in our ribs and took all the bed for himself."

"That was the king — that is the way he plays at being fierce. Say: "*Komm, Herr Jesus, und sei unser Gast,*" then draw up the stools. Ah-h . . . what have we to eat?"

The little boys shouted the answer all together: "Schnitzle — Schnotzle — and Schnootzle!"

THE BEST THAT LIFE
HAS TO GIVE

HOWARD PYLE

There was a blacksmith who lived near to a great, dark pine forest. He was as poor as charity soup; but dear knows whether that was his fault or not, for he laid his troubles upon the back of ill-luck, as everybody else does in our town.

One day the snow lay thick all over the ground, and hunger and cold sat in the blacksmith's house. "I'll go out into the forest," says he, "and see whether I cannot get a bagful of pine cones to make a fire in the stove." So off he stumped, but could find no cones, because they were all covered up with white. On into the woods he went, farther and farther and deeper and deeper, until he came to a high hill, all of bare rock. There he found a clear place and more pine cones scattered over the ground than a body could count. He filled his basket, and it did not take him long to do that.

But he was not to get his pine cones for nothing: click! clack! — a great door opened in the side of the hill, and out stepped a little dwarf, as ugly as ugly could be, for his head was as big as a cabbage, his hair as red as carrots, and his eyes as green as a snake's.

"So," said he, "you are stealing my pine cones, are you? And there are none in the world like them. Look your last on the sunlight, for now you shall die."

Down fell the blacksmith on his knees. "Alas!" said he, "I did not know

THE BEST THAT LIFE HAS TO GIVE

"No," said the dwarf, "it is too late to do that now. But listen, you might hunt the world over, and find no such pine cones as these; so we will strike a bit of a bargain between us. You shall go in peace with your pine cones if you will give me what lies in the bread-trough at home."

"Oh, yes," said the blacksmith, "I will do that gladly."

"Very well," said the dwarf, "I will come for my pay at the end of seven days," and back he went into the hill again, and the door shut behind him.

Off went the blacksmith, chuckling to himself. "It is the right end of the bargain that I have this time," said he.

But, bless you! he talked of that horse before he had looked into its mouth, as my Uncle Peter used to say. For, listen: while his wife sat at home spinning, she wrapped the baby in a blanket and laid it in the bread-trough, because it was empty and as good as a cradle. And that was what the dwarf spoke of, for he knew what had been done over at the blacksmith's house.

But the blacksmith was as happy as a cricket under the hearth; on he plodded, kicking up the soft snow with his toes; but all the time the basket of pine cones kept growing heavier and heavier.

"Come," said he, at last, "I can carry this load no farther, some of the pine cones must be left behind." So he opened the basket to throw a parcel of them out. But —

Hi! how he did stare! for every one of those pine cones had turned to pure silver as white as the frost on the window-pane. After that he was for throwing none of them away, but for carrying all of them home, if he broke his back at it, and upon that you may depend.

"And I had them all for nothing," said he to his wife; "for the dwarf gave them to me for what was in the bread-trough, and I knew very well that there was nothing there."

"Alas," said she, "what have you done! the baby is sleeping there, and has been sleeping there all the morning."

When the blacksmith heard this he scratched his head, and looked up and looked down, for he had burned his fingers with the hot end of the bargain after all. All the same, there was nothing left but to make the best that he could of it. So he took two or three of the silver pine cones to the town and bought plenty to eat, and plenty to drink, and warm things to wear into the bargain.

At the end of seven days up came the dwarf and knocked at the black-smith's house.

"Well, and is the baby ready?" said he, "for I have come to fetch it."

But the blacksmith's wife begged and prayed and prayed and begged that the baby might be spared to her. "Let us keep it for seven years at least," said she, "for what can you want with a young baby in the house?"

Yes, that was very true. Young babies were troublesome things to have about the house, and the woman might keep it for seven years since she was anxious to do so. So off went the dwarf, and the woman had what she want-ed, for seven years is a long time to put off our troubles.

But at the end of that time up came the dwarf a second time.

"Well, is the boy ready now?" said he, "for I have come to take him."

"Yes, yes," says the woman, "the boy is yours, but why not leave him for another seven years, for he is very young to be out in the world yet?"

Yes, that was true, and so the dwarf put off taking him for seven years longer.

But when it had passed, back he came again, and this time it did no good for his mother and father to beg and pray, for he had put off his bargain long enough, and now he was for having what was his.

"All the same," says he to the blacksmith, "If you will come after five years to the place in the woods where you saw me, you shall have your son, if you choose to take him." And off he went with the lad at his heels.

Well, after five years had passed, the blacksmith went into the forest to

find the dwarf and to bring back his son again.

There was the dwarf waiting for him, and in his hand he held a basket. "Well, neighbor," says he, "and have you come to fetch your son again?"

Yes, that was what the blacksmith wanted.

"Very well," says the dwarf, "here he is, and all that you have to do is to take him." He opened the basket, and inside were a wren, a thrush, and a dove.

"But which of the three is the lad?" says the blacksmith.

"That is for you to tell, neighbor," says the dwarf.

The blacksmith looked and looked, and first he thought it might be the wren, and then he thought it might be the thrush, and then he thought it might be the dove. But he was afraid to choose any one of the three, lest he should not be right in the choosing. So he shook his head and sighed, and was forced at last to go away with empty hands.

Out by the edge of the forest sat an old woman spinning flax from a distaff.

"Whither away, friend?" said she, "and why do you wear such a sorrowful face?"

The blacksmith stopped and told her the whole story from beginning to end. "Tut!" said the old woman, "you should have chosen the dove, for that was your son for sure and certain."

"There!" said the blacksmith, "if I had only known that in the first place it would have saved me so much leg wear," and back he went, hot-foot, to find the dwarf and to get his son again.

There was the dwarf waiting for him with a basket on his arm, but this time it was a sparrow and a magpie and a lark that were in it, and the blacksmith might take which of the three he liked, for one of them was his own son.

The man looked and looked, and could make nothing of it, so all that he could do was to shake his head and turn away again with empty hands.

Out by the edge of the forest sat the old woman spinning. "Prut!" says she, "you should have chosen the lark, for it was your son for sure and certain. But listen; go back and try again; look each bird in the eyes, and choose where you find tears; for nothing but the human soul weeps."

Back went the man into the forest for the third time, and there was the dwarf just as before, only this time it was a sparrow and a jackdaw and a raven that he had in his basket.

The man looked at each of the three in turn, and there were tears in the raven's eyes.

"This is the one I choose," said he, and he snatched it and ran. And it was his son and none other whom he held.

As for the dwarf, he stood and stamped his feet and tore his hair, but that was all he could do, for one must abide by one's bargain, no matter what happens.

You can guess how glad the father and mother were to have their son back home again. But the lad just sat back of the stove and warmed his shins, and stared into the Land of Nowhere, without doing a stroke of work from morning till night. At last the father could stand it no longer, for, though one is glad to have one's own safe under the roof at home, it is another thing to have one's own doing nothing the livelong day but sit back of the stove and eat good bread and meat; for the silver pine cones were gone by this time, and good things were no more plentiful in the blacksmith's house than they had been before.

"Come!" says he to lazy-boots one day, "is there nothing at all that you can do to earn the salt you eat?"

"Oh, yes," said the lad, "I have learned many things, and one over at the dwarf's house yonder, for the dwarf is a famous blacksmith." So out he came from behind the stove, and brushed the ashes from his hair, and went out into the forge.

"Give me a piece of iron," says he, "and I will show you a trick or two worth the knowing."

"Yes," says the blacksmith, "you shall have the iron; all the same I know that it is little or nothing that you know about the hammer and the tongs."

But the young fellow answered nothing. He made a bed of hot coals, and laid the iron in it.

"Here," said he to his father, "do you blow the bellows till I come back, and be sure that you do not stop for so much as a wink, or else all will be spoiled." So he gave the handle into the blacksmith's hand and off he went.

The old man blew the bellows and blew the bellows, but the dwarf over in the forest knew what was being done as well as though he stood in the forge. He was not for letting the lad steal his tricks if he could help it. So he changed himself into a great fly, and came and lit on the blacksmith's neck, and bit him till the blood ran; but the blacksmith just shut his eyes tight, and grinned and bore it, and blew the bellows and blew the bellows.

By and by the lad came in, and the fly flew away. He drew the iron out of the fire, and dipped it in the water, and what do you think it was? Why, a golden tree with a little golden bird sitting in the branches, with bright jewels for its eyes.

The lad drew a little silver wand from his pocket, and gave the tree a tap, and the bird began to hop from branch to branch, and to sing so sweetly that it made one's heart stand still to listen to it.

As for the blacksmith, he just stood and gaped and stared, with his mouth and eyes as wide open as if they never would shut again.

Now there was no king in that country, but a queen who lived in a grand castle on a high hill, and was as handsome a one as ever a body's eyes looked upon.

"Here," says the lad to his father, "take this up to the queen at the castle yonder, and she will pay you well for it." Then he went and sat down back of the stove again, and toasted his shins and stared at nothing at all.

Up went the blacksmith to the queen's castle with the golden bird and the golden tree wrapped up in his pocket-handkerchief. Dear, dear, how the queen did look and listen and wonder, when she saw how pretty it was, and heard how sweetly the little golden bird sang. She called her steward and bade him give the blacksmith a whole bag of gold and silver money for it, and off went the man as pleased as pleased could be.

And now they lived upon the very best of good things over at the black-smith's house; but good things cost money, and by and by the last penny was spent of what the queen had given him, and nothing would do but for the lad to go out and work a little while at the forge. So up he got from back of the stove, and out he went into the forge. He made a bed of coals and laid the iron upon it.

"Now," says he to his father, "do you blow the bellows till I come back," and off he went.

Well, the old man took the handle and blew and blew, but the dwarf knew what was going on this time, just as well as he had done before. He changed himself into a fly, and came and lit on the blacksmith's neck, and dear, dear, how he did bite! The blacksmith shut his eyes and grinned, but at last he could bear it no longer. He raised his hand and slapped at the fly, but away it flew with never a hair hurt.

In came the lad and drew the iron out of the fire and plunged it into the water, and there it was a beautiful golden comb that shone like fire. But the lad was not satisfied with that. "You should have done as I told you," said he, "and have stopped at nothing; for now the work is spoiled."

The blacksmith vowed and declared that he had not stopped from blow-ing the bellows, but the lad knew better than that; for there should have been a golden looking-glass as well as the comb. The one was of no use without the other, for when one looked in the golden looking-glass, and combed one's hair with the golden comb, one grew handsomer every day; and the lad had intended both for the queen.

"All the same," said the old man, "I will take the golden comb up to the castle;" and it did no good for the lad to shake his head and say no. "For," says the father, "old heads are wise heads; and the queen will like this as well as the other." So up to the castle he would go, and up to the castle he went.

But when the queen saw the golden comb her brows grew as black as a thunder-storm. "Where is the looking-glass?" said she; and though the old man vowed and declared that no looking-glass belonged with the comb, she knew a great deal better. So, now, the blacksmith might have his choice; he should either bring her the looking-glass that belonged to the golden comb or bring her that which was the best in all the world. If he did neither of these he should be thrown into a deep pit full of toads and vipers.

Back went the old man home again and told the lad all that had happened from beginning to end. And then he wanted to know what he should do to get himself out of his pickle.

Well, it was no easy task to make what the queen wanted; all the same, the lad would try what he could do. So he rolled up his sleeves and out he went into the forge and laid a piece of iron upon the bed of hot coals.

This time he would not trust the old man to blow the bellows for him, but took the handle into his own hand and blew and blew.

The dwarf knew what was happening this time as well as before. He changed himself into a fly and came and sat on the lad's forehead, and bit until the blood ran down into his eyes and blinded him; but the lad blew the bellows and blew the bellows.

First the fire burned red, and then it burned white, and then it burned blue, and after that the work was done.

Then the young man raised his hand and struck the fly and killed it, and that was an end of the dwarf for good and all.

What he had made he dipped into the water and it was a gold ring, nothing less nor more. He took a sharp knife and drew charms upon it, and inside of the circle he wrote these words:

"WHO WEARS THIS SHALL HAVE THE BEST THAT THE WORLD HAS TO GIVE."

"Here," said the lad to his father, "take this up to the queen, for it is what she wants, and there is nothing better in the world."

Off marched the old man and gave the ring to the queen, and she slipped it on her finger.

That was how the blacksmith saved his own skin; but the poor queen did nothing but just sit and look out of the window, and sigh and sigh.

After a while she called her steward to her and bade him go over and tell the blacksmith's son to come to her.

There sat the lad back of the stove. "Prut!" said he, "she must send a better than you if she would have me come to her." So the steward had just to go back to the castle again and tell the queen what the lad had said.

Then the queen called her chief minister to her. "Do you go," said she, "and bid the lad come to me."

There sat the lad back of the stove. "Prut!" said he, "she must send a better than you if she would have me come to her."

Off went the minister and told the queen what he had said, and the queen saw as plain as the nose on her face, that she must go herself if she would have the lad come at her bidding.

There sat the lad back of the stove. And would he come with her now?

Yes, indeed, that he would. So he slipped from behind the stove and took her by the hand, and they walked out of the house and up to her castle on the high hill, for that was where he belonged now. There they were married, and ruled the land far and near. For it is one thing to be a blacksmith of one kind, and another thing to be a blacksmith of another kind, and that is the truth, whether you believe it or not.

And did the queen really get the best in the world? Bless your heart, my dear, wait until you are as old as I am, and have been married as long, and you will be able to answer that question without the asking.

THE STORY OF A CAT

MARY DE MORGAN

Once there lived an old gentleman who was a very rich old gentleman, and able to buy nearly everything he wanted. He had earned all his wealth for himself by trading in a big city, and now he had grown so fond of money that he loved it better than anything else in the world, and thought of nothing except how he could save it up and make more. But he never seemed to have time to enjoy himself with all that he had earned, and he was very angry if he was asked to give money to others. He lived in a handsome house all alone, and he had a very good cook who cooked him a sumptuous dinner every day, but he rarely asked anyone to share it with him, though he loved eating and drinking, and always had the best of wine and food. His cook and his other servants knew that he was greedy and hard, and cared for nobody, and though they served him well because he paid them, they none of them loved him.

It was one Christmas, and the snow lay thick upon the ground, and the wind howled so fiercely that the old gentleman was very glad he was not obliged to go out into the street, but could sit in his comfortable armchair by the fire and keep warm.

"It really is terrible weather," he said to himself, "terrible weather"; and he went to the window and looked out into the street, where all the pavements were inches deep in snow. "I am very glad that I need not go out at all, but can sit here and keep warm for today, that is the great thing, and I shall have some ado to keep out the cold even here with the fire."

He was leaving the window, when there came up in the street outside an old man, whose clothes hung in rags about him, and who looked half frozen. He was about the same age as the old gentleman inside the window, and the same height, and had grey, curly hair, like his, and if they had been dressed alike anyone would have taken them for two brothers.

"Oh, really," said the old gentleman irritably, "this is most annoying. The parish ought to take up these sort of people, and prevent their wandering about the streets and molesting honest folk," for the poor old man had taken off his hat, and began to beg.

"It is Christmas Day," he said, and though he did not speak very loud, the old gentleman could hear every word he said quite plainly through the window. "It is Christmas Day, and you will have your dinner here in your warm room. Of your charity give me a silver shilling that I may go into an eating-shop, and have a dinner too."

"A silver shilling!" cried the old gentleman, "I never heard of such a thing! Monstrous! Go away, I never give to beggars, and you must have done something very wicked to become so poor."

But still the old man stood there, though the snow was falling on his shoulders, and on his bare head. "Then give me a copper," he said; "just one penny, that today I may not starve."

"Certainly not," cried the old gentleman; "I tell you I never give to beggars at all." But the old man did not move.

"Then," he said, "give me some of the broken victuals from your table, that I may creep into a doorway and eat a Christmas dinner there."

"I will give you nothing," cried the old gentleman, stamping his foot. "Go away. Go away at once, or I shall send for the policeman to take you away."

The old beggar man put on his hat and turned quietly away, but what the old gentleman thought was very odd was, that instead of seeming distressed he was laughing merrily, and then he looked back at the window, and called out some words, but they were in a foreign tongue, and the old gentleman could not understand them. So he returned to his comfortable armchair by the fire, still murmuring angrily that beggars ought not to be allowed to be in the streets.

Next morning the snow fell more thickly than ever, and the streets were almost impassable, but it did not trouble the old gentleman, for he knew he need not go out and get wet or cold. But in the morning when he came down to breakfast, to his great surprise there was a cat on the hearthrug in front of the fire, looking into it, and blinking lazily. Now the old gentleman had never had any animal in his house before, and he at once went to it, and said "Shoo-shoo!" and tried to turn it out. But the cat did not move, and when the old gentleman looked at it nearer, he could not help admiring it very much. It was a very large cat, grey and black, and had extremely long soft hair, and a thick soft ruff round its neck. Moreover, it looked very well fed and cared for, and as if it had always lived in comfortable places. Somehow it seemed to the old gentleman to suit the room and the rug and the fire, and to make the whole place look more prosperous and cosy even than it had done before.

"A fine creature! a very handsome cat!" he said to himself; "I should really think that a reward would be offered for such an animal, as it has evidently been well looked after and fed, so it would be a pity to turn it away in a hurry."

One thing struck him as very funny about the cat, and that was that though the ground was deep in snow and slush outside, the cat was quite dry, and its fur looked as if it had just been combed and brushed. The old gentleman called to his cook and asked if she knew how the cat had come in, but she declared she had not seen it before, and said she believed it must have come down the chimney as all the doors and windows had been shut and bolted. However, there it was, and when his own breakfast was finished the old gentleman gave it a large saucer of milk, which it lapped up not

125

greedily or in a hurry, but as if it were quite used to good food and had had plenty of it always.

"It really is a very handsome animal, and most uncommon," said the old gentleman, "I shall keep it awhile and look out for the reward"; but though he looked at all the notices in the street and in the newspapers, the old gentleman could see no notice about a reward being offered for a grey and black cat, so it stayed on with him from day to day.

Every day the cat seemed to his master to grow handsomer and handsomer. The old gentleman never loved anything but himself, but he began to take a sort of interest in the strange cat, and to wonder what sort it was — if it was a Persian or a Siamese, or some curious new sort of which he had never heard. He liked the sound of its lazy contented purring after its food, which seemed to speak of nothing but comfort and affluence. So the cat remained on till nearly a year had passed away.

It was not very long before Christmas that an acquaintance of the old gentleman's came to his rooms on business. He knew a great deal about all sorts of animals and loved them for their own sakes, but of course he had never talked to the old gentleman about them, because he knew he did not love anything. But when he saw the grey cat, he said at once —

"Do you know that this is a very valuable creature, and I should think would be worth a great deal?"

At these words the old gentleman's heart beat high. Here, he thought, would be a piece of great luck if a stray cat could make him richer than he was before.

"Why, who would want to buy it?" he said. "I don't know anybody who would be so foolish as to give any money for a cat which is of no use in life except to catch mice, when you can so easily get one for nothing."

"Ah, but many people are very fond of cats, and would give much for rare sorts like this. If you want to sell it, the right thing would be to send it to the Cat Show, and there you would most likely take a prize for it, and then

126

someone would be sure to buy it, and, it may be, would give a great deal. I don't know what kind it is, or where it comes from, for I have never seen one the least like it, but for that reason it is very sure to be valuable."

Upon this the old gentleman almost laughed with joy.

"Where is the Cat Show?" he asked; "and when is it to be held?"

"There will be a Cat Show in this city quite soon," said his acquaintance; "and it will be a particularly good one, for the new Princess is quite crazy about cats, and she is coming to it, and it is said that she doesn't mind what she gives for a cat if she sees one she likes."

So then he told the old gentleman how he should send his name and the cat's name to the people who managed the show, and where it was to be held, and went away, leaving the old gentleman well pleased, but to himself he laughed and said, "I don't think that old man thinks of anything on earth but making money. How pleased he was at the idea of selling that beautiful cat if he could get something for it!"

When he had gone, the grey puss came and rubbed itself about its master's legs, and looked up in his face as though it had understood the conversation, and did not like the idea of being sent to the show. But the old gentleman was delighted, and sat by the fire and mused on what he was likely to get for the cat, and wondered if it would not take a prize.

"I shall be sorry to have to send it away," he said; "still, if I could get a good round sum of money it would be a real sin not to take it, so you will have to go, puss; and it really was extraordinary good luck for me that you ever came here."

The days passed, and Christmas Day came, and again the snow fell, and the ground was white. The wind whistled and blew, and on Christmas morning the old gentleman stood and looked out of the window at the falling snow and rain, and the grey cat stood beside him, and rubbed itself against his hand. He rather liked stroking it, it was so soft and comfortable, and when he touched the long hair he always thought of how much money he

THE STORY OF A CAT

should get for it.

This morning he saw no old beggar man outside the window, and he said to himself: "I really think they manage better with the beggars than they used to, and are clearing them from the town."

But just as he was leaving the window he heard something scratching outside, and there crawled on to the windowsill another cat. It was a very different creature to the grey cat on the rug. It was a poor, thin, wretched-looking animal, with ribs sticking through its fur, and it mewed in the most pathetic manner, and beat itself against the pane. When it saw it, the handsome grey puss was very much excited, and ran to and fro, and purred loudly.

"Oh, you disgraceful-looking beast!" said the old gentleman angrily; "go away, this is not the place for an animal like you. There is nothing here for stray cats. And you look as if you had not eaten anything for months. How different to my puss here!" and he tapped against the window to drive it away. But still it would not go, and the old gentleman felt very indignant, for the sound of its mewing was terrible. So he opened the window, and though he did not like to touch the miserable animal, he took it up and hurled it away into the snow, and it trotted away, and in the deep snow he could not see the way it went.

But that evening, after he had had his Christmas dinner, as he sat by the fire with the grey puss on the hearthrug beside him, he heard again the noise outside the window, and then he heard the stray cat crying and mewing to be let in, and again the grey and black cat became very much excited, and dashed about the room, and jumped at the window as if it wanted to open it.

"I shall really be quite glad when I have sold you at the Cat Show," said the old gentleman, "if I am going to have all sorts of stray cats worrying here," and for the second time he opened the window, and seized the trembling, half-starved creature, and this time he threw it with all his might as hard as he could throw. "And now there is an end of you, I hope," he said as he heard it fall with a dull thud, and settled himself again in his armchair, and the grey puss returned to the hearthrug, but it did not purr or rub itself against its master.

Next morning, when he came down to breakfast, the old gentleman poured out a saucer of milk for his cat as usual. "You must be well fed if you are going to be shown at the show," he said, "and I must not mind a little extra expense to make you look well. It will all be paid back, so this morning you shall have some fish as well as your milk." Then he put the saucer of milk down by the cat, but it never touched it, but sat and looked at the fire with its tail curled round it.

"Oh, well, if you have had so much already that you don't want it, you can take it when you do," so he went away to his work and left the saucer of milk by the fire. But when he came back in the evening, there was the saucer of milk and the piece of fish, and the grey cat had not touched them. "This is rather odd," said the old gentleman; "however, I suppose cook has been feeding you."

Next morning it was just the same. When he poured out the milk the cat wouldn't lap it, but sat and looked at the fire. The old gentleman felt a little anxious, for he fancied that the animal's fur did not look so bright as usual, and when in the evening and the next day and the next, it would not lap its milk, or even smell the nice pieces of fish he gave it, he was really uncomfortable. "The creature is getting ill," he said, "and this is most provoking. What will be the use of my having kept it for a year, if now I cannot show it?" He scolded the cook for having given it unwholesome food, but the cook swore it had had nothing. Anyhow it was growing terribly thin, and all day long sat in front of the fire with its tail hanging down, not curled up neatly round it, and its coat looked dull and began to come out in big tufts of hair.

"Now really I shall have to do something," said the old gentleman, "it is enough to make anyone angry! No one would believe that this could be a prize cat. It looks almost as wretched as that stray beast that came to the window on Christmas Day." So he went to a cat and dog doctor, who lived near, and asked him to come in and see a very beautiful cat which had nothing the matter with it, but which refused to eat its food. The cat's doctor came and looked at the cat, and then looked very grave, and shook his head, and looked at it again.

"I don't know what sort of cat it is," he said; "for I never saw any other like it, but it is a very handsome beast, and must be very valuable. Well, I will leave you some medicine for it, and I hope you may be able to pull it round, but with these foreign cats you never know what ails them, and they are hard to cure."

Now the day was close at hand when the cat should have been sent to the show, and the old gentleman was getting more and more uneasy, for the grey cat lay upon the rug all day and never moved, and its ribs could almost be seen through its side, so thin had it grown. And oddly enough the old gentleman, who had never cared for anyone or anything in his life except himself, began to feel very unhappy, not only because of not getting the money, but because he did not like to think of losing the cat itself. He sent for his friend who had first told him about the Cat Show, and asked his advice, but his friend could not tell him what to do with it.

"Well, well," he said, "this is a bad business, for I have told everyone that you are going to exhibit a most extraordinarily beautiful cat, and now this poor creature is really fit for nothing but the knacker's yard. I think, maybe, some naturalist would give you a good price for its skin, as it is so very uncommon, and if I were you I should kill it at once, for if it dies a natural death its skin won't be worth a brass farthing." At these words the grey cat lifted its head, and looked straight into the old gentleman's face, as if it could understand, and for the first time for many a long year, the old gentleman felt a feeling of pity in his heart, and was angry with his friend for his suggestion.

"I won't have it killed," he cried; "why, I declare, though it does seem

131

absurd, I have lived with this creature for a year, and I feel as if it were my friend, and if it would only get well and sit up on the hearthrug, I shouldn't mind about the money one bit!"

At this his friend was greatly astonished, and went away wondering, while the old gentleman sat by the fire and watched the cat lying panting on the rug.

"Poor pussy, poor old pussy!" he said, "it is a pity that you can't speak and tell me what you want. I am sure I would give it to you." Just as he spoke there came a noise outside, and he heard a mewing, and looking through the window he saw the same thin ugly brown cat that had come there last Christmas, and it looked as thin and wretched as ever. When she heard the sound the grey cat stood up on her tottering feet and tried to walk to the window. This time the old gentleman did not drive it away, but looked at it, and almost felt sorry for it; it looked almost as thin and ill as his own grey puss.

"You are an ugly brute," he said, "and I don't want you always hanging about; still, maybe you would be none the worse for a little milk now, and it might make you look better." So he opened the window a little, and then he shut it and then he opened it again, and this time the brown cat crawled into the room, and went straight to the hearthrug to the grey puss. There was a big saucer of milk on the hearthrug, and the brown cat began to lap it at once, and the old gentleman never stopped it.

He thought as he watched it, that it grew fatter under his eyes as it drank, and when the saucer was empty he took a jug and gave it some more. "I really am an old fool," he said; "that is a whole penny's worth of milk." No sooner had he poured out the fresh milk than the grey cat raised itself, and sitting down by the saucer began to lap it as well, as if it were quite well. The old gentleman stared with surprise. "Well, this is the queerest thing," he said. So he took some fish and gave it to the strange cat, and then, when he offered some to his own puss, it ate it as if there was nothing the matter. "This is most remarkable," said the old gentleman; "perhaps it was the company of a creature of its own sort that my cat needed, after all." And the grey cat purred and began to rub itself against his legs.

So for the next few days the two cats lay together on the hearthrug, and though it was too late to send the grey cat to the show, the old gentleman never thought about it, so pleased was he that it had got well again.

But seven nights after the stray cat had come in from outside, as the old gentleman lay asleep in bed at night, he felt something rub itself against his face, and heard his cat purring softly, as though it wanted to say "goodbye". "Be quiet, puss, and lie still till the morning," he said. But when he came down to have his breakfast in the morning, there sat the brown tabby, looking fat and comfortable by the fire, but the grey cat was not there, and though they looked for it everywhere, no one could find it, though all the windows and doors had been shut, so they could not think how it could have got away. The old gentleman was very unhappy about it, but he looked at the strange cat on his hearth and said, "it would be unkind now to send this poor thing away, so it may as well stay here."

When she heard him speaking of its being unkind, his old cook burst out laughing. "Perhaps," she said, "'twas a fairy cat, as it could get away through bolts and locks, and nothing but a fairy could have taught my master to think of a thing being unkind or not. I only hope that now he'll think of someone in this world besides himself and his money." And sure enough from that time the old gentleman began to forget about his money, and to care for the people about him, and it was all the doing of the strange cat who had come from no one knew where, and gone away to no one knew where.

THE LAST DREAM OF THE OLD OAK TREE

HANS CHRISTIAN ANDERSEN

English version by Neil Philip

At the edge of the wood, on a cliff above the seashore, stood an old oak tree. It was three hundred and sixty-five years old. But years to a tree are like days to us. We are awake in the day, and asleep at night, and that's when we dream, but a tree is different. A tree is awake for three seasons of the year, and it is only in winter that it sleeps. Winter is the night after the long day that is called spring, summer, and autumn.

Many a warm summer's day the mayflies danced lightheartedly around the tree, and if ever one of them took a moment's rest on a leaf, the tree would say, "Poor little thing! Just one day is your whole life! How short a time you have. It's so sad."

"Sad?" the mayfly would answer. "What do you mean by that? Everything is perfect. It's so warm and lovely, and I'm quite happy."

"But only for one day, and then it's all over."

"All over!" said the mayfly. "What do you mean? Won't you be here?"

"Oh yes, I shall live for thousands of your days, and my day is a whole year long — longer than you could understand."

"No, I don't understand. You may live thousands of my days, but I have thousands of moments to be happy in. Do you think all the beauty in the world will die when you do?"

"No," said the tree, "I expect it will go on, longer than I can understand."

"Well, then, you and I have the same time as each other; we just reckon it differently."

And the mayfly danced and flirted in the air, delighted with its lovely wings, and the scents on the air from the clover in the fields, the roses in the hedgerows, the elder trees, and honeysuckle, cowslips, and wild mint. Their perfume was so strong that the mayfly was quite drunk with it. It was a long, beautiful day, full of happiness, full of joy. When the sun finally set, the little fly felt tired from all that fun. Its wings couldn't carry it any longer. Ever so gently, it drifted down onto the soft grass. Its head began to nod, and it fell into a happy sleep. That was death.

"Poor little mayfly," said the oak tree. "What a short life that was!"

Every summer it was the same story. The same dance, the same conversation, the same outcome. Whole generations of mayflies lived and died, and each was as happy and carefree as the first. The oak tree stayed awake through the spring morning, summer afternoon, and autumn evening. Then winter drew near. Soon it would be time to sleep.

Already the storms were singing, "Good night! Sleep tight! Shed your leaves! Pluck one, pluck two! Off with those leaves, let us ruffle your branches, we'll make you creak with pleasure. Sleep well, sleep tight, this is your three hundred and sixty-fifth night. You're still a youngster really. Sleep. Snow is falling, it will keep your toes warm. Sweet dreams!"

Now the oak tree's branches were bare, and it was ready for bed. It would sleep the whole winter long, and dream many dreams, full of adventure just like human dreams.

Once it had been tiny, with an acorn cup for its cradle. By human reckoning it was well into its fourth century. It was the biggest and finest tree in all the forest. It grew so high above the others that sailors out at sea used it as a landmark — not that it gave a thought to all the eyes that strained to make it out.

When the leaves were green, wood pigeons made their nests right at the top of the tree; in autumn, when the leaves turned to burnished copper, migrating birds rested there on their journey. But in the winter the tree was bare, and only crows and jackdaws rested in its branches, chattering about the lean times to come, with food so hard to find.

It was at the holy Christmastime that the oak tree dreamed its loveliest dream. It went like this.

In its dream, the tree knew that it was a special day. It could hear the church bells ringing, and it was a beautiful day, as soft and warm as summer. The tree unfolded its great crown, fresh and green, and let the sun play on its leaves and branches. The air was scented with herbs and flowers, and butterflies were playing hide-and-seek and mayflies were dancing as if the whole world had been made just for them to enjoy.

Everything that the tree had seen and known over its long life paraded by. It saw knights and ladies riding through the wood with feathers in their hats and hawks on their wrists. It heard the huntsman's horn and the belling of the hounds. It saw enemy soldiers pitch camp beneath its branches. The soldiers sang, and their weapons glittered in the light of the watch-fires. Then it saw two shy lovers carve their initials in its bark.

Once, many years ago, a wandering musician had hung his harp in the trees branches. Now it was hanging there again, and playing in the wind. The wood pigeons cooed for pleasure, and the cuckoo called out all the days of summer.

The tree felt life surging through it like a wave, from the ends of its roots to the tips of its branches. It basked in the warmth. It felt itself growing stronger, and taller, growing up and up towards the blissful heat of the sun.

Now it was so tall that it rose high above the clouds, which swam below it like flocks of swans.

Each of its leaves could see, as if they were so many eyes. And even though it was daytime, the bright stars came out, and winked at each other, so kind and calm they reminded the tree of the children and the lovers whose eyes had shone and sparkled beneath its boughs.

It was a moment of pure joy.

Yet something was missing. The tree wished that all the other trees and bushes and flowers could rise up too, and share its happiness. For the great oak tree could not enjoy its glorious dream to the full without the others. This wish quivered through it from top to toe, as strong as any human desire.

The tree craned down to look below. It smelled the woodruff, and then the strong scent of violet and honeysuckle. It even thought it could hear the cuckoo call.

Now the tops of the other trees broke through the clouds. They, too, were growing. The bushes and flowers were so eager in their flight that some of them pulled themselves right out of the earth. The birch soared past like a bolt of lightning. The whole forest was flying up into the sky — even the brown reeds. The birds were there, too, and a grasshopper who sat on a ribbon of grass, fiddling away on his shinbone. The songs of all the birds and insects lifted triumphantly up to heaven.

"But where are the little blue flowers from the stream?" asked the oak. "They should be here. And the harebells, and the daisies!" For the oak wanted them all to come.

"Here we are! Here we are!" came the answer.

"And what about last summer's woodruff, and the lilies-of-the-valley from the summer before that — where are they? And the wild apples, with their lovely blossom? All the beauty of the forest over all the years — if only it could be here."

"Here we are! Here we are!" came the response from up ahead.

"Oh, it's too good to be true!" cried the oak tree. "They're all here, big and little — not one has been forgotten. How can such happiness be?"

"In heaven, it can be," came the reply.

139

The tree felt its roots slip from the earth.

"That's right!" it shouted. "Now there's nothing to hold me back. I can fly up into the light and the glory, and all that I loved is with me."

"All!"

That was the oak tree's dream. And while it was dreaming on that Christmas Eve, a fierce storm raged over land and sea. The waves crashed against the cliff, and — just as the tree dreamed that its roots were loosening their hold — the wind tore the tree from the earth and it fell to the ground. Its three hundred and sixty-five years were now as a day is for the mayfly.

By Christmas morning the wind had fallen, and the sun was shining. The church bells were ringing out, and from every chimney — even from the poorest cottage — blue smoke was rising in thanksgiving like the tribute from a druid's altar. The sea grew calmer and calmer, and on board the big ship that had weathered the storm just off the coast, all the flags were being hoisted for Christmas.

"The tree is gone! The big old oak tree, that we used as a landmark!" cried the sailors. "It must have fallen in the storm. What shall we use now? There's not another like it."

That was the old tree's funeral sermon — short, but heartfelt.

The tree itself lay stretched out on the snow beside the beach. Over it washed the sound of a carol from the ship, as the sailors sung of the joy of Christmas, and Christ who was born to give us eternal life.

> Now let us of our blessings sing,
> *Alleluia, alleluia,*
> Let the song to heaven ring,
> *Alleluia, alleluia.*

So ran the old carol, and everyone on the ship was uplifted in his own way by prayer, just as the old oak tree was uplifted in its last, loveliest dream that Christmas Eve.